Mary Botham Howitt

Which is the Wiser

People abroad - a tale for youth

Mary Botham Howitt

Which is the Wiser
People abroad - a tale for youth

ISBN/EAN: 9783337082246

Printed in Europe, USA, Canada, Australia, Japan

Cover: Foto ©Andreas Hilbeck / pixelio.de

More available books at **www.hansebooks.com**

WHICH IS THE WISER:

OR,

PEOPLE ABROAD.

A TALE FOR YOUTH.

BY MARY HOWITT,

AUTHOR OF
"STRIVE AND THRIVE," "HOPE ON! HOPE EVER!" "SOWING AND REAPING,"
"WHO SHALL BE GREATEST," &c. &c. &c.

NEW-YORK:
D. APPLETON & COMPANY,
443 & 445 BROADWAY.
1863.

WHICH IS THE WISER;

OR,

PEOPLE ABROAD.

———————

CHAPTER I.

A GERMAN PICTURE.

THERE had been a deal of sorrow in the dwelling of the widow Hoffmann—much sorrow and many tears; there had been deaths of little children, and deaths also of those growing up to man's and woman's estate; there had been the destruction of all life's hopes and prospects, in the death, whilst yet in the prime of life, and the bright promise of fortune, of a beloved and affectionate husband. Add to all this, that there had been the change from plenty and prosperity, to narrow economy and the privation of every costly indulgence, and every one will grant that the widow Hoffmann was not without cause for tears; that it was not without cause either, that her once bright eye was dimmed, and her once abundant black hair was thin and of a silvery whiteness. Still, though all this was true, the heart of the widow had ceased to mourn as one without hope; and the sorrow which had passed, and which had been so overwhelming in the passing, might be compared now to the background to a picture, serving in a great degree to throw the near and the present into stronger and clearer lights.

True it is, that as the year brought round its many

memorable anniversaries (for Mrs. Hoffmann, like all
Germans, religiously kept all anniversaries)—the day
of her betrothal, five-and-thirty years before—the day
of her marriage—the birthdays of her deceased husband, or those of her numerous children—or those
darker days which the deaths of so many loved ones
had made ineffaceable in her soul—her brow wore a
more thoughtful, nay, almost a pensive character,
and she began the day with the persuasion that she
must sit down, and meditate, and be sad.   On such
occasions, however, there never failed to be an unusual mildness and kindness in her tone and manner,
and her little maid, Benedicta, otherwise Bena, who
had now lived with her nearly three years—a short,
neat, and rosy-faced German girl—never failed to
receive some mark of kindness or consideration from
her hands; in return for which, whenever she saw her
mistress unusually thoughtful, she moved about the
four rooms, which constituted the whole of the
widow's dwelling, with much more quietness than
might have been expected from any German maid-
servant whatever.

"Bena," said Mrs. Hoffmann, on a certain 6th of
June, in the year 1836, "you have been a good girl
to-day, and have remembered my orders, nor have
slammed the doors, as you commonly do, which was
very considerate; for you must have seen how bad
my head has been."

Bena smiled and looked pleased, and played with
the corner of her apron.   "And therefore, my good
girl," continued her mistress, "you shall take some
of those little cakes to your lame brother; and, if
your grandfather wishes for another bottle of wine,
he can send word.   Now go, my good girl; but you
must be back by half-past nine.   I will get my own
supper to-night; but be sure when you come back

not to ring at all violently; my head has been bad all day, and that bell alarms me so much."

Bena was the happiest servant-maid in all Heidelberg. She took the little cakes which her mistress gave her, and put them carefully into her smart holiday basket: she then bestowed upon her smooth brown hair an extra brushing, and pinned up again the back plait with more than ordinary care; for it was, she knew, a fine warm evening, and everybody would be either walking out, or looking from their windows; and Bena, although only a poor maid-servant, had a little female love of admiration. This arrangement of her hair being made to her satisfaction, she pinned about her neck a closely-plaited muslin frill, over which she tied a printed pink handkerchief, and then, putting on a clean buff printed apron, she took the little holiday basket, with its two bows of rose-coloured ribbon, on her arm, and, giving good heed to shut her own bed-room door with great quietness, set forth towards her home, which, fortunately for her, lay on exactly the other side of the city. Bena was very happy that evening; she was so glad that she had nothing to do but to walk through the whole length of that cheerful Haupt Strasse, or High Street, and that she might even look into the shop-windows if she pleased, and fancy, as she stood before a milliner's, how she should look in a bonnet, if she were only a lady to wear one; and then, after her walk was done, what a pleasure it would be to sur-prise the poor lame Peter with the delicious little cakes, which should be all for his own eating. Such were her thoughts as she quietly closed the great door of the general staircase of that large house, in which her mistress was one of the third story inmates.

This 6th of June, then, be it understood, was one of the widow Hoffmann's anniversaries, and she was willing for this evening to be alone, that she might sit and meditate. She was not, however, so wholly absorbed by her personal feelings, as not to listen for the departure of the little maiden; and even after the house-door-bell had sounded, upon her going forth, she thought for a few moments upon the patient young invalid, to whose feeble appetite she had now furnished a small enjoyment. From this she went on to think that, since the linking fast of all family ties was good for our human hearts, so should the kind little Bena not fail, on many an evening of this coming summer, to visit her family, and carry with her small presents to her lame brother and her bedridden grandfather. "It will be a pleasure," thought she, "henceforth to do kindnesses; for if, please God, that Karl pass his examination with honour, as I am sure he will, how happy shall I be! and when one is happy, then is the time to make others so. I might even now, reasoned she with herself, spite of all that I have gone through, have done much more to make those about me happy; but, Heaven help us! sorrow is such an absorbing feeling, it makes us so selfish; but if it please God that all goes on now well about poor Karl, I will do my endeavour to amend!" Good Mrs. Hoffmann, she did not know that these very sorrows of which she spoke, had opened wide her heart to every kindly sympathy, and that, if ever there was a self-forgetting good Christian, it was herself: nor was she at all aware that her kind, tender, good-will overflowing soul never was so penetrated through and through with universal charity, as on those particular days which she consecrated to her past sorrow.

The truth was, Mrs. Hoffmann reasoned about nothing, and least of all would she have thought of reasoning about herself; therefore she never came to the true conclusion, that she was a very excellent woman. Her son Karl, however, knew it well enough; and, if anybody could have persuaded her of the existence of many virtues, it would have been he; but then, Karl did not argue with his mother about anything; and, if he had tried to persuade her that she was as good as he knew her to be, she would only have answered, "Thou art partial, dear Karl; yet, for this I cannot blame thee. Thou and I are alone in the world together, and, God knows what would become of me without thy love!"

But this is the 6th of June, we must remember; and Bena has been gone these five minutes, and Mrs. Hoffmann has settled herself on the sofa, and has placed her knitting-basket on the tea-table before her, and commenced her knitting and her thinking at the same moment.

"Ah!" thought she, with a deep sigh, "five-and-thirty years is it this very day since our betrothal; and, strange enough, this day combines in itself two other memories—the death of my first-born, and, saddest of all, fifteen years afterwards, the death of that child's beloved father!—Three anniversaries in one!" The widow wept, and dwelt for some time with inexpressible anguish on the memory of this last event, and on the consequences which it had involved. But there was a golden light within her own mind which, unconsciously to herself, gleamed over all, and made her much more willingly dwell on the good things that were left, than on those that had departed for ever; therefore she thought on Karl, and dried her tears, and again resumed her knitting. Before long, her mind had gone back five-and-thirty years, and she was with her father and mother in the abode of her youth;—her father, the pastor of a rich village in the north of Germany, emphatically the father of his flock, and her mother, the *beau-ideal* of a good wife and mother—tender, loving, prudent, self-forgetting, frugal, and industrious. She remembered the winter-spinning, and the summer-knitting; the house-presses full of linen and wearing apparel; the domestic regularity, plenty, and hospitality; the almost absurdly small income, yet the never-experienced want; and she thought it was a privilege which in her youth she had never sufficiently felt, to have been the child of such parents. But as her immediate business was with one particular anniversary, she recalled the first introduction of the youth Hoffmann, the son of the rich Hamburgh merchant, into their house as her father's pupil. How vividly came back the recollection of all those times. She was sitting with her mother under the lime-tree in the front, shelling pease, on the first evening of his arrival; and there now came back to her mind the very humming of the bees in the flowers of the lime-tree above their head, and the song of the blackbird which hung in its wicker cage on the front wall of the house. Then what a golden happy time were the next twelve months!—the nativity of her soul, as it were; for until she had known Hoffmann, she had thought of little else but household cares and duties. Till then had she prided herself most on the endless variety of cakes, small and great, which she could manufacture; and on the frugal yet ever-varied dinners which she could cook; on the seventy-five pairs of stockings which she had already knit and marked, and which lay among piles of excellent wearables, all duly marked likewise and numbered, in her chest of drawers; on the bed-covers she had quilted, and on the two last winters' spinning, which enabled her to reckon among her own personal property sundry table-cloths and napkins, every thread of which had passed between her own fingers. " Ah! well," thought Mrs. Hoffmann, "it was a useful part of my education after all—a good initiation into the duties of after life—and, to my latest day, I shall have cause to bless the good mother who never allowed my hands to remain idle!"

For some time after this the knitting went on with renewed energy, but by and by it slackened into a mere mechanical movement of the fingers, as her mind reverted again to that day five-and-thirty years —the day of her betrothal. It was a happy household festival, the betrothal of an only child to a well-known youth of the fairest promise. There was almost more of a festival in it than in the marriage itself. There were two grandfathers and one grandmother present, many aunts, and uncles, and cousins near and remote; there were garlands of flowers hung on the walls; music and dancing for the youth; · plenty of wine and beer and good tobacco for the old gentlemen, and tea and cakes for the ladies! The moment when Mrs. Hoffmann's thoughts were thus far away in North Germany, and she was living over again a happy event, which lay even far more remotely in the past, she was suddenly recalled to present realities by a gentle, yet so persevering a tapping at her door, as made her instantly conclude the knock had been repeated. Immediately, therefore, on her replying, " Herein," or walk in, the door opened, and the slender, somewhat carefully dressed figure of Madame Von Holzhäuser presented herself. Who, our readers will naturally say, was Madame Von Holzhäuser? We will endeavour to satisfy their curiosity.

Madame Von Holzhäuser, then, thirty years before, was the *prima donna* of one season—the admired, nay, almost worshipped star of musical Germany

Her life, from her very cradle, had been strange and
unhappy. In her childhood she had belonged to
wretchedly poor people, who were connected with
the theatre in Berlin; her parents they certainly
could not have been, for she was subjected by them
to every possible want and misery. Her earliest
recollection was of standing at the theatre-doors to
beg, and of being forbidden, on pain of severe punish-
ment, from returning home, unless she brought with
her money to above a certain amount.

She was born with extraordinary musical faculties;
fortunately, however, this was not discovered by the
persons who had possession of her, early enough for
her to be exhibited as an infant prodigy: to them she
was useful only to beg; but many and many a night
she forgot her miserable duty—forgot even the painful infliction which was the certain consequence of
such a neglect, in listening to the glorious strains of
some favourite singer, from the half-open doors of the
opera. Occasionally, also, she crept in unobserved,
or was permitted to enter by some good-natured,
music-loving door-keeper, who, sympathising in the
wretched child's passion for his favourite art, over-
looked the small, but otherwise all-important fact, of
her having neither money nor ticket.

But at length her musical powers made themselves
known to her possessors, and then, to a certain
degree, her state amended itself. She was apprenticed
to a professor of music, who undertook to give her
all the needful instruction, on condition of sharing
with her owners the product of her first three years
of public life. She now became to them an object
of the most intense interest, and the most unsparing
pains were taken to urge her dawning powers forward.
Time was hardly permitted for sleep; day and night,
night and day, her one occupation went forward.

Now she was flattered and caressed, and promised the most splendid advantages, the most brilliant and triumphant career, whilst baubles and trumpery finery were heaped upon her as present rewards and as earnests of what was to be; then again, on the other hand, was she threatened with unimaginable punishments, and made even to suffer bitter cruelties, as a foretaste of what her fate should be did she dare to disappoint the expectations of her task-masters. But the miserable, once half-starved, and even now ill-used Marie, was one of God's noblest creatures, endowed with the rare gift of genius; and, spite of hardships and oppressions, and a moral infliction which could not be called training, she grew up with powers which promised to satisfy all the expectations of her masters, and with qualities of heart and soul which, spite of uncertainty of temper and waywardness of will, were calculated to make social life and character perfectly happy. But poor Marie belonged to that class of beings who, one knows not why, seem born to be unhappy—their business in this world is to bear and suffer—to be encouraging examples to others—to teach others patience and contentment: their reward, and their happiness assuredly, however, will come, though perhaps only in the other world.

She made her *début* in the musical world in a new opera at Vienna, and her success was instantaneous. The public voice was at once loud in her praise; princes and grand dukes listened to her with rapture, and showered upon her golden proofs of their applause; and poets, among whom was the greatest in Germany, even Goëthe himself, not only sang hymns in her praise, but gave her tokens of their devotion also. Among the very last valuables which the poor Marie parted with in her after troubles, was a ring set with one small but exquisite diamond, the gift of this noble poet.

Marie's powers had at once become as a mine of gold to her possessors, and she was watched over with the most dragon-like jealousy. She lived in splendour; she appeared in public apparelled nobly; she was seen in the streets of the city seated like a queen in a costly equipage, but she was for all this no more free than the captive in his dungeon. It was in vain that she made efforts to free herself at once from her captors; they were too artful for her, and had entangled too many snares about her for her readily to escape. For a whole season she reigned triumphant, and there seemed outwardly no probable limit to her influence and prosperity. There was, however, all this time, one deep and serious cause of doubt and anxiety both in her mind and in the minds of her masters. The severity and hardships of her earlier youth, and perhaps, also, some natural weakness in the organs of her voice, rendered the utmost care needful to preserve it, not only in its full tone and power, but also to prevent her losing it altogether. The least exposure to a damp atmosphere occasioned temporary loss of voice; but most of all was it influenced by the state of her own mind. She was often nervous and timid to a painful degree, and at such times she could not make herself audible; the very dread of such an occurrence increased the cause, and the poor *prima donna*, in the midst of the most brilliant success, was devoured by a secret fear which stung her almost to madness. To lose her voice was to lose at once her hold on the public heart, and to lose this was to be thrown back into the merciless hands of her disappointed possessors. As it always happens that there is a party against as well as for any popular person or thing, so was there also in her case; she had her opposition party, who watched her not less narrowly than her friends, with a *prima donna* elect in their hands, whom they waited impatiently to elevate upon her vacant throne. The fact of her uncertain voice was bruited abroad, and day after day they proclaimed to the public how impossible it was it could sustain itself to the end of the season. But the end of the season came, and Marie's voice did not fail her, and her triumphant partisans clapped their hands and talked loud of the brilliant certainty of the future.

Before the commencement, however, of her second season, Marie, partly with the determination to be free, and partly blinded by inexperience and affection, married, although yet scarcely nineteen. A very short time sufficed to prove that she had only diversified her misfortunes, not by any means removed them. Her husband was an unprincipled adventurer, who, by the advantages of a handsome person, good address, and real or skilfully assumed love of Marie's art, had manœuvred himself into her affections. Her affections, however, she had given him, and, at once boldly asserting herself free, she tore herself from the shackles of her former possessors, and threw herself on the protection of her husband. Alas! this was only the beginning of sorrows, and from this time forth her fate was sealed.

The second season came, and with it fervent expectation on the one hand, and more violent opposition on the other. But who can tell the secret despondency which filled her heart on the first night of that fatal second season, when she became doubtful of her own powers? On the second night it was impossible for her to present herself, for her voice was gone; but the public received the plea of sudden illness with the sincerest sympathy: there was some little consolation in that: still, night after night went on, and Marie could not sing. The new *prima donna* of the opposition party was clamoured into popularity, and poor Marie's assumed illness became real. For some weeks the public solicitude kept alive its interest in her; before long, however, they began to suspect that the servant of their pleasure was, as rumour said, no longer capable of administering to it; and it became necessary that she herself should give the best of all refutations, by again exhibiting unabated powers before them. Full of cruel anxiety and doubt, and but half recovered from sickness, Marie again made her appearance in public; all the world crowded to hear her; but the suspicion was true—she could not sing; the once glorious voice had lost its power. The public exhibited less of sympathy with her than of disappointment; and, with eyes overflowing with tears, and a heart torn with bitter apprehensions, she had the mortification, as she left the house, to hear her rival received in her stead with thunders of applause. The career of the poor, dispirited singer was at an end.

Nothing can be conceived more melancholy than the reaction of mind on the loss of public favour, under any circumstances; but in the case of this unhappy young creature it was doubly so. She had not lost the favour of the public through any crime or caprice of her own, but through an accumulation of misfortunes which her friendless, unhappy condition alone had brought upon her. From the brilliant world of Vienna, and all her courtly and wealthy admirers, she sank at once into poverty and insignificance, and found herself thus, at the age of twenty, a wife and a mother, with no earthly means of subsistence but her own exertions. So much of her life was well known to all the music-loving world of thirty years ago. The unfortunate singer was a subject of conversation for a few months; but, as she passed from the public eye, she passed also from the public heart, and was forgotten.

In many circumstances of human life the very force and irresistibleness of misfortune brings its own remedy. So it is probable was the case with poor Marie. Ten years afterwards, she was recognised by a family in Leipzig who had lived formerly in Vienna. She was then a teacher of singing by the hour, having in great measure recovered her voice, and being acknowledged one of the best teachers in the place, although her large family, her indolent, sickly husband, and her own feeble health, kept her always poor. Ah! it was unknown and unimagined, in the houses of the wealthy and well-fed, when the thin, anxious countenance of the poor singing-mistress made its appearance, how sparely she had often dined; nor, when the well-clothed and luxurious scorned her because of her long-worn and homely apparel, how carefully that apparel was kept—was kept, in truth, merely to go abroad in. They knew nothing of the feeble attempt at self-imposition, by which she tried to think that the gown really was not quite so shabby when worn, as when closely inspected; that such and such a fracture, which time alone had made, might, with a little care, be kept out of sight; or that the bonnet might do a few weeks longer, at least with new strings; and that, after all, the parents thought more of the progress of the pupil than of the dress of the teacher; and that, in fact, these clothes must do longer, inasmuch as she could not afford to buy new ones!

Poor Marie! and thus it was, that as she became shabbier in her appearance, her pupils became fewer and fewer, and belonged still more and more exclusively to the bürger class; and at last, spite of her industry and her determined integrity, poverty again came upon her like an armed man; and once more, as was ever the case in her darkest times, she lost her voice.

Nearly twenty years after this, about the time at which this our little tale opens, Marie, then more properly to be called Madam, or Mrs. Von Holzhäuser— for her husband, however unworthy, was of a noble family—had sunken into the almost old-looking woman, although in truth not fifty years of age, and had then been known as singing-mistress in Heidelberg for about four years. She had come there on the recommendation of some residents of influence, to whose family, during their summer stay in one of the lesser bathing-towns, she had given singing lessons. She brought with her an extremely infirm husband; her children—those at least that remained—were scattered here and there, and she was, like one doomed to be unhappy, wearing at that very time mourning for a son who had been killed in a student-duel at Giessen. Poor woman! she hardly ever could meet a student, with his long hair, moustachoed lip, and folio under his arm, without tears; and yet she came to live in a city of students—and why? because she had an ailing, helpless husband to maintain, and because, in this city of students, she was promised the influence of a family which might amend the prospects of her future life. All that her willingly-hopeful mind prayed for, however, did not immediately fall out; she remained poor: still that occurred to her, which for many years, nay, which for nearly all the years of her life, had not occurred before—she found some disposed to become her personal friends. External show operates much less on social life in a small city than in a rich and luxurious one; and thus many a wife and mistress of a family in Heidelberg, many hundred-fold richer than the poor singing-mistress ever hoped to be, might be seen walking abroad very little if at all better dressed than she; and, to her surprise, she found herself now and then invited, not for the sake of her singing powers, but out of perfect good fellowship and kindness, to join in many of those little summer excursions which the good Germans are so fond of making; sometimes to some favourite spot a few miles from the city, and sometimes to the castle gardens, where the ladies drank tea or coffee, the gentlemen wine, or perhaps beer; the ladies knit and talked, and the gentlemen smoked and talked also; where they breathe the fresh air, pay their few kreutzers each, and go home again refreshed in body and mind, and with their hearts warmed with good-will towards each other.

The simple fact of feeling herself not excluded from the more respectable part of society, produced a most happy effect on the mind of the poor singing-mistress. She never in the whole course of her life had experienced so much self-satisfaction, so much quiet and peace of mind, as during these latter years; and, had it not been for still lingering anxieties about those absent children of whom she said so little, and daily, never-ceasing care for her peevish and hopelessly sick home-companion, it is very uncertain whether she would not have pronounced herself really happy.

Among the kindest and best esteemed of her friends was the widow Hoffmann, whose son Karl, himself a good musician, and devotedly attached to the art, had first heard her giving singing-lessons in the house of one of his friends, but whose more intimate know-ledge of her was gained in another way. At the house of the same friend, on one damp November morn-ing, her voice again deserted her: he happened to

come in at the time, and the poor singing-mistress,
with tears in her eyes, explained to him the distressing calamity which had befallen her, and which, thus
at the commencement of winter, filled her with inexpressible alarm.   Karl was a medical student, and at
once, independently of his regard for her on account
of her musical powers, became interested in her as a
sufferer from disease.   Cheered by his kindly sympathy, the poor woman opened to him her heart; told
him of her discouraging prospects, of her poverty,
and thus her inability to pay skilful physicians.   Karl
gave his medical advice; he was young and sanguine,
and she caught at once the happy infection of his
spirit, and persuaded herself that he could do her
good; her heart was cheered, and in a few weeks,
spite of a severe January, she was able to resume her
labours.

In his capacity of medical adviser, he was admitted
into the privacy of her two small rooms—those poor,
ill-furnished rooms, into which none entered but herself, her sick husband—who indeed never was absent
from them—and those even poorer than themselves.
Karl was familiar with the dwellings of the common
poor, and he knew how heart-rending is their desti-
tution, especially in sickness; but never had he entered an abode of even absolute want, which affected
him as did the simple aspect of these two rooms—the
room of the musician without the instrument.   Mrs.
Von Holzhäuser seemed immediately to divine his
thoughts.   "You wonder," said she, "to see no
instrument; but it is long since I had pupils at home;
my husband could not bear it; I have long ceased to
play for my own amusement: besides, I have not
time, for, setting aside the daily lessons I give, I
copy a good deal of music," said she, turning towards
a small table where she had evidently but lately been

so employed. "It comes cheaper than the printed notes, and many of my pupils prefer it on this account." Hoffmann did not know at that time that many hours were stolen from sleep, to add, by this means, some little to the daily income. How much patient striving against poverty and misfortune is there in this world, of which the next-door neighbour knows nothing!

The more Hoffmann saw of this praiseworthy woman, the higher rose his esteem for her. He prescribed for her ailments, and for those of her husband; he talked cheerfully to the ill-tempered invalid, and accomplished in his case what his wife had believed totally impossible; he induced him now and then to leave his room, to look more cheerfully on life, to acknowledge that his wife did all that lay in her power for his comfortable maintenance, and even to make a half-promise that some time or other, at least if he got better, he would himself copy music.

By degrees the two rooms, if they were not better furnished, assumed a more cheerful aspect. A contented countenance contributes more to the cheerful aspect of a room than the finest furniture; and thus, although the large, ill-dressed person of the Herr Von Holzhäuser might be often seen half obtruded through the small third-story window, with his long pipe in his mouth, yet he was not now always looking down, as though in ill-humour with all the world below.

Things evidently were mending with the Von Holzhäusers; their health improved, more money came in, and a better moral tone pervaded the mind both of husband and wife; nor did a day pass in which Mrs. Von Holzhäuser failed to breathe inwardly, if it was not expressed aloud, a blessing on the excellent young man who, not only by the exercise of his skill as a physician, but by the high moral

tone of his own nature, wrought so wholesome yet so
silent a change. Her health was better than it had
been for years; and in the bright days of the June of
which we are now writing, she might be seen, when
extraordinary occasions called for so much display,
dressed in a real new gown, real new black silk
mode, and a bonnet but little the worse for wear.
It was thus apparelled that, after having knocked
twice at the widow Hoffmann's door, she entered the
room, interrupting, as we said a few pages before,
reminiscences which were likely to become somewhat
too gloomy.

Mrs. Von Holzhäuser seated herself on the sofa by
her friend; and, after many inquiries as to each other's
health, and mutual assurances that it gave them great
pleasure to know that each was so well, Mrs. Hoffmann went on with her knitting, talking cheerfully all
the time. When all available topics of personal interest had been gone through, Mrs. Von Holzhäuser
went on to say, that she had been sent for this
morning by the English lady, who lived in the second
story, and who wished her to give singing-lessons
to her daughter.

"And a very pretty girl that is," said Mrs. Hoffmann; "I have met her on the stairs occasionally,
and have seen her frequently, these warm evenings, in
the balcony below. The mother I have not seen."

"She appears to be in very weak health," said
Mrs. Von Holzhäuser; "she lay on the sofa, supported by cushions, and wrapped in large shawls,
although the weather is now so warm."

"Poor creature!" said Mrs. Hoffmann.

"She said," continued the other, "that she had
been at the baths last autumn, on account of her
health, having left England for that purpose; that
they had spent the winter in München, and had

intended this summer to return to England, but had altered their plans in consequence of some rich relations, or acquaintance, I forget which, who had promised to spend some time with them in Heidelberg, if they could obtain for them sufficiently handsome apartments."

" So !" remarked Mrs. Hoffmann, with very expressive emphasis.

" Her daughter, she says," continued Mrs Von Holzhäuser, " is so charmed with the neighbourhood, and with the castle, that she wishes to remain here six months, which she has consented to do, especially as she has taken the whole suite of apartments below for that time, for this great English family, who spend, she assures me, their money like princes."

" I wish such English people would not come here," said Mrs. Hoffmann, in a tone of undisguised disgust; " they do us great mischief. We might as well have an army of French, laying waste and despoiling our houses and vineyards, as these troops of frivolous, money-loving, money-wasting English. Germany, dear, home-loving Germany, has more deep and grave cause of fear from these smiling, flattering, yet deriding visiters, than from a whole nation of Frenchmen with arms in their hands !"

" You do not like the English," quietly remarked her visiter.

" I do not like the English as we see them in Germany," said Mrs. Hoffmann; " they love dissipation more than enjoyment; they value money not for the good it will do, but for the show it will make; they think to pass here for princes, and they only make themselves the laughing-stock of our people; and yet even upon those very people their moral influence is bad. You are right; I do not like the English !"

" I cannot afford," said Mrs. Von Holzhäuser, " to dislike the English, whatever their faults may be, so long as they pay me. It is true that I have given singing-lessons but in very few English families. They like, as you say, to pay high prices—they can afford it; but my misfortunes," added she, with a sigh, " have ever prevented me having high prices."

" Get what you can from the English," said her friend, smiling, " since they are so fond of what is dear; they will like you all the better for it, and I wish you a hundred such pupils!"

" But this English lady below," replied Mrs. Von Holzhäuser, " is not, after all, one of the class you speak of. She inquired my terms strictly—appeared to like them better for their moderation—made me sit down and give her proof of my ability to teach. I had to sing Italian, French, and German, before she made up her mind even to my moderate terms."

" Dear Heaven!" exclaimed the other, in her old tone of disgust.

" There was nothing so unreasonable in that," said Mrs. Von Holzhäuser, with a sigh; " the young lady offered me wine, but it is too hot for wine, so I accepted a glass of water. She speaks excellent German; the mother spoke French; and, after all, I came away by no means displeased; and to-morrow morning from eleven to twelve I give my first lesson. But now," resumed she, after a pause, " I want to know something about Karl. When will this examination be over; and what tidings have you from him?"

Mrs. Hoffmann laid down her knitting, which through the whole of the previous conversation she had pursued with most persevering assiduity, and at once began to look anxious and deeply interested. " I shall have a letter to-morrow: the examination will be over by that time. I shall now have him back in a few days. Poor Karl, it is a mercy he has kept his health."

"How happy he will be! how happy you will be!" said poor Mrs. Von Holzhäuser, reverting with painful remembrance to her own unhappy son. At that very moment the door of the room suddenly opened, and the little Bena, looking very hot and happy, presented herself and a letter at the same moment.

"It is a letter from Carlsruhe," said she; "I knew you would like to hear it. I told them at home that I would be back in no time; but the letter is from the Herr Karl!"

"Thou art a good girl!" said her mistress—using, in the fulness of her joy in seeing her son's handwriting a day before she expected, the kindest of all modes of speech to her handmaiden—"thou art a good girl, Bena; now run away to thy lame brother:" and the next moment, breaking the seal, she read aloud—

"DEAR MOTHER—Thou must know—for to whom will the tidings be so welcome as to thee?—that my examination will be over to-night. Thy son, even, is satisfied with himself.

"Von Rosenberg and Feldmann will meet me at Wiesloch. To-morrow evening I shall again be with thee. Thine, ever,

"HERMANN KARL HOFFMANN."

"Your tidings are indeed happy!" said the poor singing-mistress, with tears in her eyes.

There were tears also in the eyes of her friend—tears of affection and happiness. "Thank Heaven!" said she, Karl's examination is over; he will be back again to-morrow: but stay," added she, looking again at the letter, "he will be here to-night; this letter was written yesterday; he will be here immediately. Thank God, I am indeed happy!"

She spoke truly. She was at that moment really and thoroughly happy. Life had then no troubles—

no dark side—no mournful anniversaries! Her son, her only remaining child—the sole object of her affections and her life's cares—her pride, her glory, her hope, was returning to her with honour, after a severe states examination. She always expected it would be so, for Karl was, as everybody knew, so good, so clever, so successful in all that he did; still this certainty, this security, now all was over, seemed so much beyond the joy that she imagined, that it was no wonder she wiped her eyes before she was able to talk about her happiness; and then all at once a world of housekeeping cares overwhelmed her. He was coming back that very evening, and with him his two friends; where, then, was the fatted calf that ought to have been made ready in honour of such a guest? and where was that giddy little Bena, that happened to be now out of the way just when she was wanted? Mrs. Hoffmann, hastily giving her friend a hint of her instant perplexity, projected her head through the open casement, to see if, by good chance, the girl had met with a gossip in the street below. But no, the street was full of people, old and young, students and shopkeepers, ladies and children, and maid-servants in plenty, but the neat little Bena, in her blue dress and pink neckerchief, was nowhere to be seen; so the good woman drew herself back with the wise determination, that since there was nobody at home to do anything for her, she must do all for herself; therefore, requesting her visiter, who rose to depart, with warm congratulations on her lips, to send in from the baker, as she went by, a fresh supply of white and brown bread, and still farther, to speed a message from the said baker's to Bena, with orders for her quick return, she gave herself up to the preparation of a hasty, but by no means a scanty supper.

Good Mrs. Hoffmann! she might have been seen enveloped in a large apron, busied in her little kitchen, whose stove she speedily set alight, amid a variety of odd, little, old-fashioned, three-legged pots, and the most grotesque earthen pipkins and pans, preparing those particular dishes which she knew her son most enjoyed, and which, in her German housewifely knowledge, she thought best suited to the occasion; thinking, every now and then, with a self-reproving mind, that perhaps she had dismissed poor Mrs. Von Holzhäuser with very little ceremony, but that she must be excused for the occasion's sake, and also that ample amends should be made to her before long.

Whilst the kind-hearted German mother is, therefore, busied in her affectionate cares up in the third story, let us descend one story lower, and make the acquaintance of the English mother and daughter, of whom our poor singing-mistress has already spoken. We must see them, for they will be no inconsiderable actors in this our little story.

CHAPTER II.

FIRST GLIMPSES.

It was, as we have said, a fine balmy sunny evening, at the beginning of June—one of the loveliest evenings of an unusually lovely season. The varied tints of the vernal green had not yet sobered down into the monotonous hue of the later summer. The dark green pine woods yet shone out conspicuously above the clear green of the vineyards, and the delicate green of the birches. The Neckar, the loveliest of rivers, went flowing on, making low music over its waves, and, amid its half-sunken rocks, looking itself like liquid emerald. The noble ruins of the castle

3

were tinted with the golden light of the declining sun, and that sun itself was flooding the whole plain with a dazzling glory, glittering upon the winding course of the noble Rhine, and making the sweeping outline of the distant Hardt mountains distinctly visible.

To have seen that evening, in the little city and its immediate environs, the crowds of people who were leisurely passing along in all directions, it might have been supposed that all its inhabitants, moved by one impulse, were abroad; but the sound of music, which issued from many an open casement, or from behind the closed Venetian shutters of many a window upon which the sun yet shone, told that still some remained at home, and that, probably, youth and even beauty might be found within four walls, even on an evening like this. Such was the case, as many a one that evening passed the house of which the English lady and daughter were inmates. Their rooms, of course—they being English—were on the second or principal floor. Their sitting-room opened into a balcony, into which, within the last few weeks, a quantity of well-grown oleanders, roses, and myrtles, had been placed, giving an air of taste and elegance both to within and without. The windows were diapered and curtained with white muslin, the casements were thrown wide, and the passer-by, if he were not arrested for a second or two, at least relaxed in his speed as he went by, to listen to a voice of unusual power and sweetness, which was heard within singing, to the accompaniment of a harp, some of the most popular German songs.

"It is the young Engländerin," said the passers by; "she and her mother have been here a few weeks; she is very handsome."

"So!" exclaimed the other German—man or woman, whichever it might be—hoping that the same rich voice and sweet music might thus greet them in the words of their favourite songs, as they returned. Within this airy and pleasant room, which withal had an airiness and pleasantness very un-English in its character, sate the two ladies, who could not for half a second have been mistaken for anything but English, although the younger had been singing German songs for the last hour, and the elder had made all the passing observations during that time in French. These two were a Mrs. Palmer and her daughter Caroline, or, as she was mostly called by her mother, Lina.

Mrs. Palmer, a middle-aged, slenderly-formed lady, was reclining still on the sofa, still supported by cushions, and still enveloped in large shawls, as when Mrs. Von Holzhäuser had seen her. She had the air of one suffering between indolence and indisposition. An open letter was in her hand, at which she glanced from time to time, although she knew very perfectly every word it contained.

"Well, love," said she to her daughter, "I think you have practised enough for once. I am sorry to keep you in on such a fine evening, but, spite of this agreeable letter, I am not able to walk to-night."

"You are not worse, I hope, dear mother," said Caroline.

"No love, no," replied she, "but the letter excited me, and I always suffer from excitement."

"But they are really coming now," said her daughter; "and, as it is all so comfortably arranged about the rooms, there need be no more vexation about it. Seven rooms all upon this floor, and three of them so handsome—they must be satisfied; and, even if they are expensive, that matters nothing."

"Certainly not," replied the mother, turning again to the letter, "the Wilkinsons never think of money

tnese are her own words, 'We must have from seven
to ten rooms'—now, there are seven rooms here, and
very good sized too—' the style and rent of which we
leave entirely to you. You know, however, what we
have always been used to. Mr. W. cannot bear a
low room, and I love one in which my friends can be
seen to advantage.'"

" I can fancy I hear Mrs. Wilkinson saying that,"
said Caroline, interrupting her mother, and smiling.

" ' This is of more importance,' " continued Mrs.
Palmer, still reading from the letter, "' than the value
of a few pounds. A few hundreds more or less make
but little difference at the year's end.' She always
was so generous!" exclaimed Mrs. Palmer, with
enthusiasm.

"The truth is, mamma," said Caroline, laughing,
" she never knew the want of money."

" ' But,' " continued the mother, reading again from
the letter, "' one thing is indispensable—our lodgings
must be near yours. I wish you to be with us every
day, and all day long. We are tired of the gaieties
of this place, and we want to ruralize in good company. Arthur Burnett, as I think I told you in my
last, joins us in Switzerland, so that he will be with
us during our entire stay in Germany, and will make
us much better worth entertaining while with you.
I hear great things of Caroline's beauty. You must
take care that her complexion is not ruined by the
horrid German stoves. A German winter, in fact, is
the destruction of female beauty.' I wonder whether
that is true," said Mrs. Palmer, abruptly laying down
the letter, and raising herself on her cushion—" it is
a shocking thing if it be; and, now I think of it, it
may be so, for one never sees a handsome woman of
thirty in Germany, while in England, on the contrary, women improve every year, often till they are

forty—at least if they grow stout at that age. I shall begin to hate Germany!"

"Well, at all events, dear mother," said her daughter, "it is not winter now, and I will endeavour, I promise you, to look my very best when the Wilkinsons are here, if that will only keep you in good humour with Germany."

"O yes, love," replied the mother; "so that you really do not suffer by these terrible stoves, I am satisfied. Germany suits me, in many respects, better than England; and if we can remain in this place, which is moderately cheap, and contrive to have a little gaiety while the Wilkinsons are here, which I am sure we may, for they love it dearly, never think of expense, but do everything so nobly! and if you can only go on with your music here, why, then, I say Germany suits me infinitely better than England. In England we could make no figure with our income; and as the Wilkinsons are so much on the continent, that is another reason; and one must confess that we have everywhere associated with the most distinguished English. You have been always very fortunate. You remember all the kindness of Sir James and Lady Ashburn, and how gay we might have been all the time at Baden; and all that cost no more than a handsome dress, which is no more than one owes to one's self. No, dear girl, you need not fear my being dissatisfied with Germany; all I want is to economize for the next six months. I care nothing for these middling people: and then we will go for the next twelve, at all events for the winter, to Dresden or Vienna."

"And perhaps," suggested Caroline, "we can persuade the Wilkinsons to go there too."

"Let me see," said her mother, turning again to the letter; "what do they say about this rich Mr Burnett?"

"That he joins them in Switzerland," said the daughter, to whom the letter had already been twice read, "and that he will help to entertain us all here."

"That he will remain with them during their entire stay in Germany," said the mother; "if, therefore, we," continued she, "find him as agreeable as he ought to be with his good income, I give you leave to use all your influence to persuade them to pass the winter where we do—or rather," said she, speaking out the real truth, "we will be guided in our future movements by theirs."

Tea was now brought in by their rosy-faced, stout, German maid; for, although Mrs. Palmer wished, unquestionably, to pass for an Englishwoman of some consideration, and as yet held in contempt the widow Hoffmann, whose rooms, in the third floor, were directly over her head, she also kept no more than one servant, and that one not a smart-dressed, capped and bonnetted, and expensive English servant, but a hard-working, strong-built, and hard-handed German girl, who submitted to be scolded by her mistress in bad German, on consideration of six pounds a year wages. As to the dinners which Mrs. Palmer and her daughter eat, it must not be supposed for a moment that they satisfied themselves with thin soup, lean beef and sour krout, and noodles, or dumplings of half a dozen different kinds—in the preparing of which consisted the sole cooking skill of Gretchen, their maid; no, the ladies were duly and daily supplied with the very best which the best *table d'hôte* of the place afforded. "This," said Mrs. Palmer, many a time, "reconciles me to Germany; how otherwise could an English lady exist here? Their common dishes are an abomination to me: the Germans want refinement, everybody must confess; think only of their undisguised, barbarous names for

things—for the very meat which one eats—to talk
of eating *flesh!* No, indeed, unless I could have
French or English cooking I must leave Germany!"
Gretchen, therefore, found, after all, her place not
to be despised. She, like every German girl, was
skilled in plaiting and arranging the hair, and this
was the sole duty she had to perform for her young
mistress, "die Fräulein Lina," for whose beauty and
excellent German she had the highest admiration;
and many and many were the five minutes which she
and the little Bena, from the third floor, gossiped
together over the goings on of the two families, and
in comparing the respective particulars in which English and German ladies resembled and differed from
each other. But, as we said before, tea being brought
in, Caroline sat down to the tea-table, which stood
before the sofa on which her mother reclined.

"And now, Lina, dear," her mother began—whose
thoughts had all this time been busied on important
matters of economy and display—"you must wear
your older dresses, for the present; at least, I mean
till the Wilkinsons come, which will not be long;
and keep your new Paris bonnet till then; you will
go out a great deal in the carriage with Mrs. Wilkinson, and you must be well dressed. I am glad we
got these singing lessons so cheap—and really how
charmingly she sings!"

"Poor lady!" said Caroline, with a sigh; "I know
not what it was, but there was something to me quite
affecting about her."

"She looks in bad health," said the mother; "on
the stage she would be rouged, and dressed up, and
look quite differently: those sort of people always
look haggard and miserable."

"She does not sing in public now," said Caroline;
"she has not sung in public for these five-and-twenty
years."

"My dear child!" remonstrated the mother, "did I not ask her about what we heard of Goëthe's admiration of her—and the diamond ring?"

"Yes," said the daughter, "and did you not observe the painful expression of her countenance? I am sure it is painful for her to remember those times. I was sorry you spoke of it: but what a beautiful voice she has! I must sing that sweet song from *Otello* with her to-morrow!—I never heard a sweeter voice in my life!"

"Well, love," replied her mother, "I hope you will profit by it. You may have three lessons a week, if you like it, for they are cheap enough—at least till the Wilkinsons come. And I am sure," continued she, after a pause, "we ought to think it a great compliment to us, that the Wilkinsons come here, to a little quiet, stupid place like this, when they might live in any city whatever in Germany, or Italy, or in Paris itself; for money is nothing to them."

"But," said Caroline, "they are tired, they say, of gaiety, and wish to ruralize; and I am sure nothing can be more charming for those who would enjoy beautiful scenery, and quiet country excursions, than this lovely neighbourhood; and the Wilkinsons, you must remember, have never been here: every scene will be new to them. But there is one thing which I must confess astonishes me, how an active, scheming, money-making man, whose head is always occupied by joint-stock banks, and joint-stock mining companies, should think not merely of coming to a place like this, but of stopping here six whole months!"

"I dare say he will not be here all the time," said the mother; "he is here, and there, and everywhere, in no time. Don't you remember his travelling post from Rome at a minute's warning, and again, only this very spring, from Florence? and now, you see, he is with them again; and yet I should not at all wonder if urgent business do not carry him off to England before they get here."

"And then," said Caroline, "their coming here will be again deferred."

"Oh, no! I should think not," returned her mother; "Mr. Burnett joins them in Switzerland; and it is my opinion that this time they will really come."

"At all events, the rooms are ready for them," said the daughter.

"But, dear me! what carriage is that that has this moment stopped?" exclaimed the mother; "surely it cannot be they; look out Lina, dear."

She rose to the window, and, quietly closing the casement, that her observation might be less obvious from without, replied, turning quietly again from the window, "Oh, no, certainly! only some students— three young men; two of them I met on the stairs the other day; they look perfectly wild—perfectly overflowing with animal spirits, and are giving a most cordial cheer to somebody at the window above;" and, feeling herself liable to observation, she withdrew quite from the window, and sat down again by the tea-table.

"Bless me, what a noisy set!" exclaimed Mrs. Palmer, as she heard the three mount up the general staircase, two steps at a time, and, with loud laughter and merry voices, pass the very door of the room where she and her daughter were sitting. Up stairs went the six noisy feet, and into the very room over Mrs. Palmer's head. The room in which she was sitting was a lofty one, and the house was well built; but the entrance of Kar. Hoffmann and his two friends into the widow's uncarpetted room, made itself distinctly audible to those who were below.

'" Surely students do not lodge in this house!" exclaimed Mrs. Palmer, "for that is what neither I nor Mrs. Wilkinson could endure!"

"No," said Caroline, "it is only the son of a Mrs. Hoffmann, who lives on the third floor, returned from his examination. Gretchen, who dearly loves to tell all the news, told me to-day, while dressing my hair, that he was coming in a day or two. According to her account he is wonderfully handsome, and so clever, and excellent, that I have a vast curiosity about him."

"They are a sad noisy set," remarked the mother, as again sounds, by no means gentle, were heard above. "One might as well have the old woman spinning overhead, like poor Mrs. Barrow, at München, as all this riot."

"By the bye," said Caroline laughing, "Gretchen says a great deal about Mrs. Hoffmann's spinning; she spins all winter, and knits all summer."

"Again!" exclaimed Mrs. Palmer, who was getting very nervous. "I never heard such a disturbance; what in the world are they doing?"

Caroline laughed aloud. "They are all drawing their chairs to the table; one hears everything so plainly on the bare floor. I am sure they are happier than common mortals to-night! The mother is a widow; she and I always exchange greetings on the staircase; she is a thorough German, though, and this son, Gretchen says, is everything that a widow's son ought to be. I cannot help being interested in his arrival. Don't you remember that sweet poem of Chamisso's?" and she repeated, in the original German, what we will give in English.

"See, father, see!—a letter! The student days are done;
They have created doctor, with high applause, thy son!
By the next post, so writes he, he will be here to dine:
Fetch, mother, from the cellar, the latest flask of wine!"

" And now he is come," said she, with heightened colour, and glistening eyes; "and how gladly would I sit down with that proud and happy mother, up stairs, even to a supper of sliced sausage, brown bread, and potato salad, could I only witness the pleasure beaming in their faces, and which, after all, is but a faint image of the pleasure of their hearts!"

" What a silly girl you are!" said the mother, smiling nevertheless; for the earnestness and sincerity with which her daughter spoke made her look really beautiful. " But I assure you, that however enthusiastic you may be about the poetry of German life, as you call it, brown bread, sliced sausage, and potato salad, would be very unpalatable to you. The want of refinement in German manners makes them perfectly repulsive to me. No English gentlewoman, I am convinced, could ever be reconciled to the habits of German women—say nothing of German men."

" I am not quite sure, dearest mamma," said Caroline, " whether, supposing it possible for one to become reconciled to those little peculiarities, one should not find some real refinement of feeling—more genuine, unwearying, unselfish kindness of heart among the Germans, than among the English of the corresponding class in society."

" How in the world can you make that out?" asked the mother.

" I think," said she—" but then I do not pretend to any great experience in life—that the English with limited incomes, those at least who have an appearance to keep up in the world, have too much necessity to care for themselves, to have much thought and feeling to expend on others, excepting inasmuch as they think and care for what others say and think about them. For instance now, Madame Von Vöhning, in Stuttgart, if she had been an English lady, could she have afforded, out of her small, miserably small income, to expend all that world of love and benevolence which lay in her heart, upon everybody about her? She would have had too much need to have spent all her love upon herself; she would have had not a single florin to spare from caps and gowns, for all those little elegant presents she bestowed upon all her friends!"

"But then," replied Mrs. Palmer, "only think of her—a woman noble by birth, noble too by marriage, living as she did! spinning and knitting, too, ever-lastingly! wearing herself those coarse, black knitted stockings! Oh, it is all very well, Lina, in old-fashioned, unrefined Germany, but such things would not do in England!"

"Certainly they would not," replied she; "but I am almost inclined to think, that this very simplicity of life, so long as it excludes none of the higher attri-butes and accomplishments of mind—and, was not Madame Von Vöhning highly accomplished, and her mind of a very high order too?—superior to all the artificialness of social life in England."

"You are talking about what you do not under-stand," said her mother; "you were a mere school-girl when we left England; you have been in Ger-many fourteen months, and yet you draw comparisons and pass judgments just as if you had the experience of a life. Now let me ask you a simple question. Do you think young men of education in England would go rioting up stairs as those three did just now? or would drag their chairs along an uncarpetted room as they are at this moment doing, to the disturbance of a whole house?—that is not so very unselfish, I think! Would educated young Englishmen do so?"

"Perhaps not, dear mother," said she; "but then

you must take into account that these very young men, if they were English, although they might enter a house with much more propriety, and lift a chair quietly across a room, especially if it were uncarpetted, would probably at the same time have so little reverence or respect for their mother as not to take supper with her at all, and most certainly not one so humble and unexpensive as a poor German widow would be able to provide. Do you remember young Venables, and his Westminster and Cambridge life?—and yet everybody said what a fine gentleman he was!"

" Yes, but," replied Mrs. Palmer, " he was a thoroughly dissipated, heartless young man!"

" Poor Mrs. Venables!" said Caroline, " and she sunk her very annuity to save him from debt and disgrace, and yet he hardly showed her common gratitude!"

" He is an extreme case," said her mother, " quite an extreme case; he was always a good-for-nothing youth. I remember him quite a boy, and as a boy he was spoiled by his poor mother: if his father had lived he would probably have been very different. He was not of a disposition to succeed under a woman's training. Yours is a very extreme case, Lina."

" It may be so," replied Caroline. " I suppose there may be such as he in Germany; but still I cannot help fancying, so long as a handsome, wonderfully accomplished young man—such, for instance, as that young Eichholz who studied at Bonn—will consent, at one-and-twenty, to wear a coat which has been turned, because his parents were not rich, and he had many brothers and sisters who also had to be clothed and provided for, that there must be more social virtue, more real stamina for unselfish character here, than with us, where so much is sacrificed to show."

" Nonsense! child," returned her mother; " you take

4

up such foolish theories! How is it possible that you can form any decided judgment on either side ?"

" I am very much of a chameleon, dear mamma," said Caroline; " I take my colouring from the influences that surround me. I remember when I first came to Germany, feeling the utmost disgust to hundreds of things which I am now reconciled to. I was then as proudly patriotic as you, and should have thought young Eichholz and his old coat ridiculous ; but, someway, one changes in feeling and opinion, one knows not how. Excellent Madame Von Vöhning, with all her quiet, sterling virtues, influenced me more than any person I ever knew; she seemed the personification of every social virtue—so simple, so true-hearted, so refined; she made even economy fascinating; and, for me to love economy, who have had more grave lectures from you on extravagance than on any other subject, is, I think, something gained."

" Very true, my dear," replied her mother; "and this I will say, that you have been much more thoughtful, in many ways, of late ; but I beseech of you not to adopt any extreme opinions. However, this I can tell you, England is the only true and fitting home for a gentlewoman ; and I shall not be pleased with your adopting any prejudices whatever. I grant, that nothing is more disgusting than that John-Bullish spirit which asserts all foreigners to be fools: they are not so : but as to my comparison between German and English social life and virtue, the case is this—England is the rich family, Germany the poor one; the advantage that the German has is, that he is contented with his poverty, and makes the best of it—that is his blessing, his philosophy, or what you will. The English, as a nation, may live freely and spend freely; the same sacrifices, the same self-denial is not required from them: in them it would be parsimony. Liberality and magnificence are their virtues! Oh, they are a fine people, the English! and I am proud to think that the Wilkinsons are as good a specimen of the nation as one would wish to see out of the four seas! I am proud of my nation, Lina!" added Mrs. Palmer, feeling very patriotic, "and so ought you to be! and I shall be very much disappointed, and it will be very much against my wishes, if you form any connexions but with your own country! I am English in all my feelings and prepossessions—so was your father: it was his boast that there was not a drop of foreign blood in his veins: he was of a good old Saxon stock, and I am sure he would have been as much distressed as I should be, that you should connect yourself with foreigners."

"Dearest mamma!" remonstrated Caroline, "you are indeed jumping to a very bold conclusion. But see, what a splendid sunset!" said she, rising from the tea-table; "will you not stand a few moments in the balcony? the air is so pleasant, and the plants make such a perfect screen from below."

Mrs. Palmer declined, saying that she would write the answer to Mrs. Wilkinson, now that all was so agreeably settled, that the letter might leave by the morning's post. Caroline drew on her gloves, and, opening her small parasol, took her stand among the flowers in the balcony.

The widow Hoffmann's three guests had by this time finished their evening meal, and, in a most German-like fashion, Karl's two friends leaned out from the open casements, enjoying the freshness of the sunset air, whilst Karl, seated by his mother on the sofa, related to her all the details of the long and arduous examination, which had, however, now terminated so happily; and because it had terminated happily, both he and she could talk over its anxieties, and he could tell her all the nervous excitement through which he had passed; the days of mental exertion which left him for some time without appetite, and without the power of sleep; and yet how his acquired knowledge, and the internal force of his own mind, had borne him up above all trial and all difficulty, and he had now returned to her with honour and applause, and with every chance of success in life bright before him.

"Thank God!" exclaimed the widow, wiping her eyes, and kissing her son's forehead.

So sat they at the very moment when Caroline rose up from the tea-table, and invited her mother to look out on the sunset; but soon after she had taken her stand alone in the balcony, hidden almost by the tall oleanders and myrtles, from the passers-by below, Karl Hoffmann also had joined his friends at the window. The windows of his mother's room looked directly down on the balcony, and the three young men were presently aware of the presence of the " fair Engländerin," who, quite unconscious of the eyes which were upon her, stood under the slanting screen of her parasol, thinking over the conversation she had just had with her mother, and feeling not at all disposed to alter her opinions. Much longer, perhaps, she might have pursued the subject, had not she been made aware of those above her, by three German words spoken by a deep, manly voice, and which evidently were applied to herself.

"A beautiful head!" said the speaker, presuming, we may suppose, that the fair English maiden did not understand the language. Caroline, without even glancing upward, withdrew from the balcony, and, standing still at the open window, enjoyed, for a full half hour, the charm and freshness of the evening. She heard nothing more spoken from the window above, but, from some cause or other, she did not forget the little compliment, but actually, the first

time she passed the mirror, glanced in it to see if the
speaker had shown good taste in his observation.

Poor Mrs. Palmer! if she had known that the
foolish Caroline listened even now with greater interest to the bustling feet above stairs—which were
heard in no silent motion, but which she was too
much occupied by her letter-writing then to notice—
she would indeed have grown angry, more especially
as towards ten o'clock, when her letter was finished,
they descended the echoing staircase in what she
pronounced a most tumultuous and ungentleman-like
manner. But had she really known that her daughter
rose to the window to see if she could then discover,
through the summer twilight, the forms of the depart-
ing young men—noisy, smoking Germans! she would
have been ready to give up her lodgings at once,
although she had just engaged seven rooms under the
same roof, for her dear English friends the Wilkinsons!

Caroline saw that only two left the house; and from
this she concluded that the widow Hoffmann's son
lived with his mother; and of this she was presently
after convinced, by hearing a firm, manly step pacing
the chamber above, and soon after, the sound of a
piano accompanying the rich voice of a very fine
singer. Karl Hoffmann was, perhaps, singing to his
mother's playing, or, what was much more likely,
was accompanying himself. He was, indeed, a good
musician: she knew the air so well, she herself sang
and played often; she thought of young Venables,
and his heart-broken mother; she thought of her own
English cousins; and then she thought of that excellent young Eichholz of Bonn, who condescended
to wear a coat which had been turned: and, while
she kissed her mother with deep affection that night,
in retiring to rest, she thought that she should hardly
become a convert to her prejudices against the Germans.

CHAPTER III.

SKETCHES OF CHARACTER.

DAYS passed on, and weeks; and, though Mrs. Palmer received duly an answer to her letter from Mrs. Wilkinson, dated München, to which city they now, accompanied by the rich Mr. Burnett, had advanced on their route from Italy, through Switzerland, avowing still "their impatience to leave gaiety and dissipation, and settle down in rural quiet amid the far-famed beauties of Heidelberg," still they came not. Mrs. Palmer, therefore, grew very nervous on the subject, and, to her daughter's alarm, seemed threatened by one of those low, nervous fevers, from which she had already suffered so much.

It was with painful anxiety that Caroline awaited, every returning day, the coming in of letters. At length a second letter came. Mr. Wilkinson had been summoned, on most urgent and important business, to Paris; he could not return to them for many weeks, as, probably, he must visit Petersburg and Vienna—his affairs were so extensive, so weighty, said his wife; and really when, as one might say, the fate almost of empires depended on a stroke of his pen, it was wonderful that he could spare any time for pleasure-taking, especially in so quiet a place as Heidelburg. She feared after all, that perhaps he might not be able to return to them, and that, perhaps, she must resign so great an indulgence as seeing her dear friends in Heidelberg, as, if Mr. W. found it necessary to go direct to Vienna, she should prefer joining him there; but, at all events, she should wait for letters from him from Paris, and be guided by them.

Poor Mrs. Palmer grew a great deal worse on reading this epistle. "Mr. Wilkinson," said she, "is unquestionably a great man, and has wonderfully extensive concerns of a money kind. He is a great banker, or something of the kind, and advances money, like the Rothschilds, to all the courts of Europe almost; but then, dear Mrs. Wilkinson ought not to let me engage expensive lodgings for them, the rent of which is now going on. Surely they will not let me be responsible for the rent!"

" Certainly not," said her daughter.

" But I assure you, dear Lina," replied Mrs. Palmer, our landlord considers me responsible; and his manners were very unpleasant to me the other day. He did not like, he said, the rooms remaining unoccupied so long; that seven applicants had been about them; and, altogether, I felt as if he wanted his money. I told him he was quite sure of his rent; and, perhaps, after all, it was only fancy. But I do not like the man; and it will be very unpleasant to have to pay a quarter's rent for those great rooms out of my own pocket, if not a whole half year's—very unpleasant, indeed! And Mrs. Wilkinson—I must say it—seems to show very little consideration for us, through the whole affair. Not one word does she say now about the rent!"

It was in vain that Caroline assured her mother, that their friends understood these things, and would not allow them to be sufferers. Poor Mrs. Palmer was nervous and out of humour, and full of suspicions; and, now that her mind was wrought up to it, she confessed to her daughter many little peculiarities in dear Mrs. Wilkinson, which proved how utterly thoughtless she was about money-matters. She was always used to so much herself, that she could not conceive other people's being short of it; and she quite believed, that if they did not come to Heidelberg, they never would think again about the lodgings, though they had been engaged by their orders; and, as to reminding them of it, it was out of the question. She had already received handsome presents both from Mr. and Mrs. Wilkinson—so had her daughter —and therefore they must stand to the responsibility, vexatious as it was.

The more Mrs. Palmer thought on the subject, the more nervous and irritable she became, till at length she appeared seriously indisposed.

"Do call in a physician for your mother," pleaded the poor singing-mistress, who now, having given Caroline three lessons a-week for several weeks, had become sufficiently familiar to venture on giving advice. "Oh, how I wish the Herr Dr. Hoffmann could see your mamma! Although he has only just taken his degree, he is so clever!" And then the good lady told over again the cases in which Karl's skill, even before he had arrived at the dignity of a doctor's degree, had wrought such miraculous cures.

Caroline sighed, and said that if her mother would but consent, a physician should be sent for; but that it must not be one young, and without experience— it must be the first physician of the place.

It was long, however—although Mrs. Palmer was decidedly a nervous patient—before she would consent to a physician being called in, and that only through the interference of a third, and very unlooked for party.

Madame Von Holzhäuser had, as we have said, given now some week's lessons to Caroline, and had in the meantime become greatly interested in her. She had so much apparent simplicity of character, seemed so natural and amiable, sung so sweetly, and had such fine talents for music, and withall so strong, or rather so willing, an admiration for the German character, and listened with such pleased curiosity to all the good lady's praise of her friends in the third story, that she declared to them, that there never was an English girl so worthy to have been born a German as Caroline Palmer.

The English lady and her daughter, as yet, had no acquaintance in the city; they were, in fact, scarcely known in it; for Mrs. Palmer, ever since she had had heard of the Wilkinsons' intentions to join them, reserved all her going abroad for their carriage, or in company with people of so much consequence as they. Caroline, too, since her mother's indisposition, had hardly left her room, so that, excepting to those who inhabited the same house—and they were but few—the young English girl was comparatively unknown. She could not help feeling her situation melancholy and forlorn; she thought, though she did not venture to say it to her mother, that Mrs. Wilkinson's conduct was heartless, or, to say the least, inconsiderate; and she did not wonder at her anxiety. How often did she wish to act on Mrs. Von Holzhäuser's suggestion, and ask advice and consolation, or at least the friendly notice, of the warm-hearted German widow in the third story. Her eyes filled with tears when she told her mother how kindly Mrs. Hoffmann had stopped her on the stairs, to inquire after her health.

"I am sure," said she, "it would do you good to see her. I wish she would bring her knitting, and sit with us."

Mrs. Palmer grew almost angry with her daughter; reproached and sighed over her dilatory, inconsiderate friend; reckoned up, for the fiftieth time, how much it must deduct from their half-year's income, if they had all this expensive suite of apartments to pay for; rang for the maid, to inquire if the postman had been to the house, only to learn that he had, but had brought no letter either for her or for her daughter; and then, half with vexation, and half from bodily indisposition, had a fit of crying, which left her with violent headache and low spirits all the rest of the day.

However much Caroline Palmer might at this time desire the friendly acquaintance of the widow Hoffmann, they, on their part, also felt towards her the most friendly sentiment. Karl, for instance, seldom went to the window without glancing down into the balcony to see if the same beautiful head, whose dark, glossy hair, he knew so well, was there among the flowers; and many a time he listened to her voice, as it rose to his ear in the melody often of his own favourite songs, through the open windows of the two floors. Mrs. Hoffmann, however, had a barrier to overleap before she could admit any active interest for the young stranger, and that was the fact of her being English. Many an argument was begun and left unfinished on national character and national prejudices; and, so determined was the good German mother against all English people whatsoever, that, had there not been another plea than that of mere beauty and general amiability—an appeal to her sympathy—Caroline might have lived seven years under the same roof, without having been vouchsafed even one word. But no sooner was the kind-hearted widow informed that the mother of the young foreigner was ill—was suffering from a nervous attack—a fretful, irritable invalid, and that as yet they had no friend in the city to whom the poor girl could look for comfort or assistance—that they had not even a physician—she forgot, at once, that she was English —forgot, in short, that she was other than one of the great Christian family, of which all men are brothers, whose duty it is to love one another; and she made up her mind to waive all ceremony, and introduce herself.

" I don't mind in this case; it is a very peculiar

one," said she to her friend, the singing-mistress; " I will go down and see if I can be of any service to them. The daughter, you say, speaks German—that is right—for I neither speak French nor English. I like neither one nation nor the other !" said she, with a smile so full of benevolence as almost to contradict her words, which, however, were the genuine sentiments of her heart. " There need be no further intimacy; but if one can be of any little service while the mother is ill, it is no more than one's duty."

Accordingly, five minutes after Mrs. Von Holzhäuser was gone, Mrs. Hoffmann put on her better gown and her visiting cap, and descended the stairs, pausing, however, a full half minute before she knocked at her fellow-inmate's door, to consider with herself whether she should not afterwards repent of what she was doing. " It is but a common neighbour's duty," said she to herself, recollecting the last Sunday's sermon on the parable of the man who fell among thieves; so she knocked, and the next moment was received by the young English girl, with such a cordial, grateful welcome, as at once set her at ease, and made her feel that she was indeed a good Samaritan.

When Karl returned home this evening at near ten o'clock, at the very moment he passed the door of Mrs. Palmer's apartments, it was opened by Caroline, who, with happy smiles, and assurances of gratitude and kindness, was taking leave of his mother. He paused for half a second and bowed; and his mother, with an instinctive feeling of pride, which ever rose to her heart at sight of him, remarked to Caroline that he was her son.

" So you have been calling on the invalid lady below," said Karl, as they both entered their sitting-room together. Mrs. Hoffmann believed it necessary, in the first place, to convince her son of the propriety of the visit she had made, taking it for granted that he must have the same scruples to English acquaintance as herself; nor did she proceed to give him any details of her call, till he had three times assured her he thought she had done quite right. She then told him that the mother really was ill—that is, out of spirits, and frightfully nervous and irritable; she pitied, she said, the poor girl extremely, who seemed amiable and modest, and well educated; that she had talked a great deal with them both, and even had persuaded the mother to let a physician be immediately sent for; that he had come while she was there; and that, altogether, she thought her visit had done them good. The physician, she said, had told her privately, that Mrs. Palmer would soon be better if she would not irritate and excite herself; that he had prescribed going out almost daily in a carriage; and that, altogether, she was pleased she had been down; although she, for her part, was determined not to begin any intimacy, for she did not admire the mother, certainly; and when these great English friends came, for whom the suite of apartments below had so long been taken, they would, evidently, be altogether too grand for her acquaintance.

The next morning Caroline made a call on Mrs Hoffmann, not only to thank her for her neighbourly attentions the night before, but also to give her the agreeable intelligence that her mother was much better this morning; which the grateful girl was quite willing to attribute to the cheerful hours she had spent the evening before.

Day after day went on, and Caroline lost no opportunity of improving an acquaintance so happily begun. Madame Hoffmann seemed to her as a second Madame Von Vöhning; and not a day passed without intercourse of one kind or other. Often she took her work and sat with her; often Karl would bring a book and read to her and her mother for hours. It was a calm and a happy time! One day Caroline was sitting alone with Mrs. Hoffmann, and they began to speak of the English friends they were expecting, and of whom every inmate in the house had already heard many rumours, although nobody, as yet, could tell anything positive about them. "They are your relations, I suppose," said Mrs. Hoffmann, who, like most other people, had some curiosity even when she was not particularly interested.

"Not relations," said Caroline, "but very old and dear friends of mamma's—Mrs. Wilkinson, at least; she and mamma were school-fellows and school-friends nearly thirty years ago, and they have been friends ever since, though it has so happened that they have not frequently met. A very kind intercourse has, however, always been kept up between them; and, now that there is a prospect of our spending three months at least with them, perhaps more, mamma naturally thinks of it with great pleasure."

"They come here from Italy," remarked Mrs. Hoffmann.

"They spent the last winter in Italy," said Caroline, "and come here by way of Switzerland. They are now in München. The continent is very familiar to them, for they have resided mostly abroad, and mostly in the large cities. Mr. Wilkinson is immensely rich, and they have the greatest possible pleasure in spending money—as much, mamma says, as he has in accumulating; and, though he has vast concerns all the world over, I have heard it said that he never made an unfortunate speculation in his life."

Mrs. Hoffmann replied by that wonderfully expressive German monosyllable, "So!"

5

Caroline thought with herself, that perhaps she had said quite enough of these unknown strangers, whom, it was not to be expected, could be interesting to Mrs. Hoffmann, but that good lady's curiosity, perhaps, was not quite satisfied, or, perhaps, out of mere courtesy, she renewed the subject, by remarking, " And Mrs. Wilkinson, I suppose, is about your mamma's age? And a very agreeable person she must be, from what your mamma has said."

" I am sure," replied Caroline, pleased with the apparent interest the other took in their expected friends, " that you will be quite charmed with Mrs. Wilkinson. Mamma thinks her one of the most delightful persons she knows. It is three years now since they met. They spent a summer together at Cheltenham. I was not with them. That summer I spent with my godmother in Ireland; and, strange as it may seem, I have seen her but twice—but how well I remember that twice! Once my nurse-maid dressed for me a very smart lady-doll, which she called Mrs. Wilkinson—for Mrs. Wilkinson's name was quite a household word; it meant whatever was munificent and generous, because, as long as I can remember, she sent me vast quantities of beautiful toys and fine presents. Of this doll I knew nothing; so when it was dressed the maid came running to me, telling me that Mrs. Wilkinson was in the drawing-room, and wanted to see me. I ran in, but when I found only the doll, my disappointment was extreme, and, I am ashamed to say, I actually tore off its clothes, and dashed the doll, which was of wax, and thus soon spoiled, on the floor. At that very moment, by some strange chance or other, the true Mrs. Wilkinson actually came in, and, poor dear lady, was so pleased and flattered by what had happened, that she gave the maid and me each a guinea, and sent us off in her carriage, she to buy a new gown, and I a new doll. You will confess that I, a little child, had reason to remember her. The next time I saw her was equally memorable to me. But I fear I I shall weary you," said Caroline; "it cannot interest you to know anything about so complete a stranger as Mrs. Wilkinson."

"No; I pray you to go on!" said Mrs. Hoffmann, most kindly, "I am interested—extremely interested; I assure you."

"The next time, then, that I saw Mrs. Wiikinson," continued Caroline, "was, as I said, equally memorable. I, being an only child, was destined to learn all that it was thought needful for me to know, from teachers at home. My godmother, a most old-fashioned lady, who approved of no modern innovations, and who, in her youth, had gone to school, and learned all kinds of needlework, and who knew, by heart, all the Psalms of David, the Collects of the Church of England—to say nothing of the Church of England Catechism—by the time she was twelve years of age, was greatly shocked at the mode of education pursued by mamma, and insisted upon my going to school. Mamma remonstrated; I cried; but, as the godmother was rich, and was expected to endow me with some of her worldly goods, it was thought best and wisest to acquiesce, and to school I was sent. The choice of the school could not have been judicious, or perhaps I, by my former mode of education, was unfitted for school. However that might be, I was very unhappy. I had always hitherto lived with those older than myself, in an intimacy, and confidence, and consideration among them—of the wisdom of which I say nothing—but which certainly had made my childhood a very happy one. At school I was at once thrown among girls, many, as I remember them, very coarse-minded, and all of them full of reckless gaiety, which made me timid, and, ignorant of school-life as I was, the butt of their never-ending ridicule and mischief. The school teachers, who themselves must have been women of very ordinary minds, and who certainly, and perhaps naturally, estimated a pupil by her showy accomplishments more than by her moral qualities, soon pronounced me both ill-tempered and stupid; and, as you may easily believe, I was very wretched."

"I can believe it, my dear young friend," said Mrs. Hoffmann, laying down her knitting, and giving her hand to Caroline, "I can believe it. Grown people often ridicule the sorrows of children; they will not believe that children can have sorrows. God knows how many a young heart aches, and how many a bitter tear young eyes shed in secret! I am no disbeliever in the griefs of children. I believe you were wretched; and, for my part, I never see a school of young ladies, even here, without a sentiment of commiseration, without my own heart being troubled. I believe that even here many a school-girl is unhappy; and how much more—pardon me for saying it—how much more must it be the case among you, where life is so much more artificial!"

Caroline's heart felt as if it were knitted to that of the widow Hoffmann, and, with tears in her eyes, she exclaimed, "I always knew, dear Mrs. Hoffmann, that you and I should be friends!"

Mrs. Hoffmann smiled, gave Caroline her hand, and remarked, "So Mrs. Wilkinson, then, relieved you from this school-bondage?"

"Yes, indeed she did," replied she; "and I shall always love her on that account. Dear me! how that melancholy six months lives in my memory! I had always been used to go out long walks with my

governess; half a day's ramble was so common to me,
that it never seemed like an indulgence. The very
week after I first went to school, what a rejoicing and
exultation there was—for the whole school was to go
out a long walk! Not a walk through the town, two
and two, beginning with the tall ones and ending
with the little ones, all paired like a regiment of
soldiers, and where, because she is nearest to you in
height, you always chance to walk with some girl you
dislike; but a real ramble into green lanes and
flowery meadows, where you might run about, or
choose your own companion; in short, it was a day
of liberty. I was the only one that did not jump
about for joy: they thought me so odd and so stupid,
and I thought them so rude and so silly, to make such
a fuss about a walk. Alas! before that day six
months, I had learnt what a source of real joy was a
country ramble to a school-girl; a pleasure which
came only twice a year; a peep, as it were, into the
world which lay beyond our narrow bounds, and our
yet narrower experience; a change from the irksome
sameness of school routine. Good Heaven! how
thankful I used to be if the governesses only changed
their seats, or wore a new gown—my mind was so
wearied with the monotony of everything about me;
therefore, though in a much quieter way than the
others, did I rejoice equally with the wildest, when the
day came for our country ramble. Yet, even in the
midst of that much-enjoyed indulgence, I went mop-
ing along in a silent sentimental state—in a melancholy day-dream—thinking how different a walk twice
a-year was, to one taken every day, and dwelling
with morbid recollection on my pleasant country
home, my mother, my governess, even my lessons at
home. We were in a woody green lane; the school
party were a long way behind, gathering nuts, or

making garlands of autumn flowers, when I came suddenly upon a gay pic-nic party which was seated in a wide, green, and shady place. What a charming, yet melancholy spectacle, was this to my eyes! I too had often gone out with my mother and her friends on such excursions. I knew exactly how one felt when seated on the grass, the horses tied to the trees around, and the gay carriages drawn up behind; it filled my young imagination with ideas of halting caravans in the desert. I easily converted horses into dromedaries; and the bright-coloured shawls, and the servants in smart liveries, gave a colouring to the picture, which was altogether oriental. How I wished I were one of the children seated there! nay, even that I was a servant to wait upon them—anything rather than a school-girl! I screened myself behind a tree, and looked on for some time, as I thought unobserved; when, all at once, a merry-faced boy, of about my own age, but a great deal stronger, sprang upon me, and, seizing one of my hands, attempted to drag me forward. I was ashamed and half frightened, whilst he, laughing, called to his sister to help him, for that I should not go until I had eaten some strawberry cream and biscuits. Strawberry cream and biscuits! what a sound it was for a school-girl! I began to cry; yes, Mrs. Hoffmann, although I was thirteen years of age, I began to cry! but whether it was at the idea of my favourite strawberry cream, or whether for shame, or fear, or envy of those happy people, I know not. By this time, however, all eyes were upon me; the ladies—several of them at least—rose from the grass and came towards me, inquiring with the utmost gentleness whence I came, and who I was; I mentioned my name, when, judge of my surprise at the exclamation of ' Good heavens! Caroline Palmer! my own little pet Lina!' and the next moment I was kissed on forehead, cheek, and lips, by kind, dear Mrs. Wilkinson. She seemed like an angel from heaven! My tears, which now flowed in torrents, from surprise and excitement, were wiped away by her delicately perfumed and embroidered handkerchief; and the next moment I was seated beside her on cushions which seemed as soft as an eastern divan, and eating strawberry cream! She began almost immediately to speak of my school-life; she said she disapproved of it altogether; that she had written many letters on the subject to my mother; and bade me tell her, was I happy? I opened all my heart; I told her all my troubles, great and small, and all the gay pic-nic party joined in saying that I was an ill-used and much-to-be-pitied child. Oh, how I loved them all!"

"But," interrupted Mrs. Hoffmann, "where were your school-companions all this time, and your governess? Surely you were sought after, inquired after."

"Yes, indeed I was," returned Caroline; "scarcely had I finished my history, and won for myself the sympathy of all my new friends, when a peasant came up and inquired if such a young lady as I had been seen; and, whilst he was being assured of my safety, the lady of the school herself, looking hot and anxious, and very angry, came also. I had been missed, but not certainly for some time after I left the school-party. They were then halting at a cottage scarcely a quarter of a mile off, where tea was ready; but my absence, I am sorry to say, had spoiled their pleasure. Some said that I had run away; some that I was lost; and others, that I had drowned myself. A long parley ensued between the mistress of the school and Mrs. Wilkinson. I do not pretend to say what would have been the most proper course to have been pursued; the one declared I should return with her to the school, and thence be dismissed to my mother, as a hopeless delinquent; the other claimed me as the child of her best friend, and declared that I never again should set foot over the school threshold.

"Mrs. Wilkinson, who never in her life has been accustomed to fail in her object, of course carried the day triumphant. I went in her beautiful carriage that night to the cottage she had taken for the summer months, ten miles off, in a gay little watering-place. She wrote to my mother that very night. I had her consent to remain a month as Mrs. Wilkinson's guest. How they managed to pacify the old-fashioned god-mother, I know not; my clothes were fetched from the school; and so ended my school-days!

" I had the honour of giving a children's ball during the month of my gay visit. I had a pony to ride, when I accompanied Mrs. Wilkinson on horseback; or I sat with her in her handsome carriage, when she made excursions into the neighbourhood, made morning calls, or went shopping; and one day—oh it was very wrong!—she actually drove to the town where I had gone to school, and went to a shop—a confectioner's shop—just opposite the school, where the carriage stood half-an-hour, on purpose that they might see how grand and how happy I was. It made me quite melancholy to look up to that school-room window, and to see the faces I knew so well, looking out. They saw me, but if they thought I exulted, they were mistaken. I was very glad when we drove away."

" Your feeling certainly was right," remarked Mrs. Hoffmann; " I respect you for it. But has Mrs. Wilkinson herself no family?"—for she was greatly interested in Caroline's sketch of character.

" They have an adopted son, or nephew—for that, I think, is the relationship they give him the benefit of," replied she, " who is to them both more than common son or daughter. Relation he certainly is not, though closely connected with the family by marriage. Mr. Wilkinson's sister married a gentleman who had one son by a former wife; he inherited a large property from his uncle, a merchant of Bristol; and, after his father's and his step-mother's death, while he was yet a boy, Mr. Wilkinson, who was, I believe, his guardian, took him to his house, and spared no expense of tutors, or anything else upon him. He was brought up at one of our great universities, and has been on the continent for the last two years. He joined them in Switzerland, and remains with them during their stay in Germany. I have not yet seen him, nor has mamma for several years. Mrs. Wilkinson, however, writes wonderful things about him."

" I hope you may find him agreeable," said Mrs. Hoffmann.

" I hope so too," said Caroline ; "for, as we are to be inmates of the same house for three months, it certainly is worth hoping for, on my part."

CHAPTER IV.

A PARTY OF PLEASURE.

IT is astonishing what an intimacy sprang up between the two small households in a short time. Karl and his mother were speaking about the Palmers one morning at breakfast, and he was expressing the greatest pleasure in their acquaintance—the first English people that he had had an opportunity of knowing at all intimately.

" I must confess that I do not augur much good from this intimacy," said Mrs. Hoffmann, who, spite of the interest she felt in Caroline, was yet beset with

misgivings and jealousies as to how the acquaintance
might in the end turn out.

" You need fear no harm from it," said Karl: " I
myself am leaving you in a few weeks; and, even
before that time, their English friends will be with
them, when, if they do not need your acquaintance,
you can so naturally drop theirs. But whilst the
mother confesses herself so much cheered by your
little attentions, and you yourself acknowledge the
daughter to be so amiable and natural, nay, so altogether charming, I cannot see any reason for your
being dissatisfied with what you have done."

" I think the mother worldly," said Mrs. Hoffmann,
" very worldly. She often, it is true, has the skill to
conceal it; but I am sure that, however much she
may say about gratitude to me for my neighbourliness,
and all that, she would be ashamed of my acquaintance before those whom she considered either her
equals or superiors; and therefore I will pursue the
acquaintance no farther. Why should I? Why should
I prepare any needless vexations for myself? That
you are going away very soon, I know, and for that
very reason I will enjoy the few weeks of your stay
in unbroken comfort. I will not be intimate with
these people, for I foresee, as plain as may be, that
one way or another it will end in trouble. I have a
foreboding in my mind against it."

Karl laughed. "A woman's argument, my dear
mother," said he, " is always one of feeling, not of
reason. You have many prejudices against all foreigners—against the English in particular: in this
instance your natural kind-heartedness has prevailed
over them; but, now that the exercise of benevolence
is no longer called for, you fall back upon your prejudices, and persuade yourself that they are founded
on reason. The truth is, that your acquaintance with

these amiable foreigners has endangered your prejudices, and now they all rise up in array, and call a
host of forebodings, equally false with themselves, to·
their aid. No, no; be guided by me: do not cast off
your new friends so abruptly; wait and see, first of
all, whether they are unworthy: if, when their rich
relations come, they no longer seek your acquaintance,
you have nothing to do but quietly to stay in your
own rooms, and let them enjoy their grandeur to
themselves; but if, as I believe, you find them
increasingly agreeable, increasingly friendly, why
should you withdraw thus voluntarily?—nay, give
them cause to think you uncertain in your disposition, even when yourself, only the last evening, acknowledged how much you enjoyed their society—
how much you were charmed with the freshness,
simplicity, and sincerity of character of the younger
lady, to say nothing of her beauty and her accomplishments."

  " Yes," said his mother, " all that I acknowledge;
but they placed me under the fascination of a spell,
as it were; my eyes are now open, and I am influenced by my reason. As long as I could do any
good, or be of any service—while, for instance, the
mother was an invalid—it was so different; but, now
I am not wanted, I cannot longer be useful to them."

  " Depend upon it," said Karl, " if you wish to do
good, you ought by no means to drop their acquaintance, for the daughter at least, if not the mother,
will be benefited by you. If I am not greatly mistaken, Miss Palmer is of a noble nature, with great
truthfulness of character—exactly such a one as will
take a life-long impression from the beauty and
nobility of virtue, especially when presented to her
through the imagination ; now her imagination is
enlisted on the side of our German virtues, do not

let her be repulsed by a noble-hearted German
woman whose friendship she solicits!"

"Oh, if I were young, Karl," said his mother, "it
might be all very well; I might then make new
acquaintances, or new friendships, but at my time of
life it is out of the question; I cannot promise even
to oblige you by keeping up this intimacy: and why,
indeed, should it oblige you? After a very few weeks
you, in all probability, will never see them again, and
when you are gone, this interchanging of visits, this
intercourse with people whose feelings, and views,
and objects in life are so different to mine, will be
irksome and unpleasant to me, and therefore I beg
you to urge me no further."

This little conversation had been more immediately
occasioned by a wish on Karl's part, that the English
mother and daughter might be invited to join a party
which, in a day or two, was going to spend the afternoon among the old castles of Neckarsteinach, a place
of favourite resort, a few miles up the valley of the
Neckar. Nothing can be imagined more charming
than this place: the noble sweep of the river; the fine
outline of the hills; the picturesque ruins of the
castles, the ancient strongholds of robber-knights, so
renowned and so terrible as to have acquired the
expressive surname of Landschaden, or Bane-of-the-
land; the more modern castle, still inhabited, and
which, with its tall towers, and picturesque gables
and galleries, its modern flower-garden, and modern
glass windows, seemed so beautifully to ally the rude,
strong grandeur of the middle ages with the elegance
and comfort of modern days and manners—the
singular old walled city of Dülsberg, on the opposite
hill, sending back the imagination to the fenced cities
of the Philistines, in the days of Joshua and the
Judges of Israel; together with the old, but beauti-

fully clean church, in which lie buried the Landschaden of far-gone generations, with effigy and
memorial stones, commemorating, in rude verse, their
proud alliances, their desperate valour, and their many
virtues: all these combined make Neckarsteinach not
only an object of interest to strangers, but of never-
ending delight to residents of the neighbourhood.

Karl Hoffmann had described the place to Caroline
and her mother the evening before; and they, who,
following the physician's advice, had driven out almost
every day, declared, after what they had heard. that
they immediately would visit so charming a place,
and not leave it, as they had hitherto intended, till
their friends the Wilkinsons would go with them. A
party of the Hoffmanns' friends were going there in
a day or two; the Hoffmanns were going with them,
and Karl's wish now was, that Mrs. Palmer and her
daughter should be invited to take half their carriage,
and thus to join what Caroline had repeatedly expressed a wish for—a real German party into the
country.

Mrs. Hoffmann, however, had got up this morning,
as we have seen, with, as she said, "her eyes
opened," and therefore she would not consent to
her son's proposition, and was furthermore bent upon
dropping the Palmers' acquaintance altogether.. But
how very little can people make sure of their own
actions! Even Mrs. Hoffmann, with all her prejudices, was a proof of this.

That afternoon a lively tap at her door, and the
customary "Herein," from herself, brought in Caroline Palmer, who, with a countenance beaming with
pleasure, came in, in the first place she said, knowing the kind interest Mrs. Hoffmann took about them,
to tell her that they that morning had received a letter
from Mrs. Wilkinson, announcing their positive arrival

6

in a very few days. "A charming letter it is," said Caroline. "It has made poor mamma quite well; and
she is now busy giving orders to two women about
the Wilkinsons' rooms being made quite ready. It
is the third time mamma has had them prepared, but
this time, I think, it will not be in vain. I feel sure
they will come—mamma thinks about Monday, as Mrs.
Wilkinson generally travels on a Sunday; she says
the country is on that day so much more lively, so
much more full of peasants, or rather the peasants so
much more visible—all smart and bright, in their
holiday dresses. Yes, I really think they will come
this time."

Mrs. Hoffmann expressed sympathy with Caroline's
hope, and she did it with sincerity; for, spite of all
she had said in the morning, the very tone of her
voice, the truthful expression of her eyes, when she
gave Mrs. Hoffmann credit for taking part in their
happiness, brought back at once all the kind sentiment she had ever felt towards her.

"And now, dear Mrs. Hoffmann," said Caroline,
"after having told you of the expected pleasure, I am
to present mamma's best compliments, and to prefer
a request in which I sincerely join. Will you and
Mr. Karl give us your company to Neckarsteinach
to-morrow afternoon? After what he said of that
sweet place, we can no longer delay a visit to it; the
carriage is already ordered; and, having thus seen it,
we shall only be the better cicerones for our friends;
but perhaps we are unreasonable; we want the
pleasure to-morrow to be made doubly great, by the
charm of agreeable companions; we want, in short,
you to go with us. Surely you will not refuse
us!" said she, laying her hand on Mrs. Hoffmann's,
in whose eye she fancied she saw the shadow of a
refusal.

Poor Mrs. Hoffmann! she knew not what to do. Two opposite feelings were at work in her mind—the will to oblige Caroline, towards whom her heart always softened, and the desire to keep up an appearance of consistency with what she had that very morning expressed to her son; but Caroline's gentle, beseeching eyes were still fixed upon her, and the acquiescence of her reply went even beyond what she herself intended.

"It is rather singular, Miss Palmer," said she, "but I and my son have had some conversation about an excursion to Neckarsteinach, but a few hours ago."

Caroline's eyes brightened.

"But I must express a little difficulty to you,' continued Mrs. Hoffmann, to whom it had instantly occurred, that perhaps Mrs. Palmer herself might object to join a German party, and that she and her son being already engaged to such a one, might thus easily hold themselves excused; "a small party of our friends have for some weeks planned an excursion to Neckarsteinach in which we have promised to join. They have fixed upon the day after to-morrow— Saturday; now, I am sorry for it, but two days successively at Neckarsteinach would be too much for me. My son proposed asking you and your mother to join the party, but all are strangers to you, excepting ourselves—all Germans; two of them young men, friends of my son's; and such a party would hardly be agreeable to you—certainly not to Mrs. Palmer."

"Am I to understand," asked Caroline, "that supposing mamma liked to join your party, that you give us an invitation to do so?"

"Certainly," returned Mrs. Hoffmann, a little perplexed by Caroline's zeal; "but I must warn you that all are Germans—and not grand people, by any means," added she, with a very peculiar smile.

"If you will allow me," said Caroline, "I will mention it to mamma, and return immediately with her answer." Mrs. Hoffmann, of course, appeared most anxious that she should do so.

"I certainly," said Mrs. Palmer to her daughter, when she had heard of Mrs. Hoffmann's proposal, " should not like to go with such a party—queerly dressed German women, and smoking German men— all coarse, ill-dressed, and odd-looking as these Germans are, if the Wilkinsons were here; but as it is, and I feel pretty sure that they will not come till about Monday or Tuesday, and you wish for it so much, I don't mind; only recollect this, that I pay for the carriage, and that nobody goes with us but the Hoffmanns: I invite them to two seats in it, and thus we shall be secure. But you must send Gretchen and postpone the order for the carriage till the day after to-morrow, unless Mrs. Hoffmann can get the party arranged for to-morrow, which would be much better, in case the Wilkinsons should come on the Saturday; do, love, try and get it so arranged; I dare say it will not matter to any one its being a day earlier, and it is of consequence to me."

When Caroline returned to the third floor, she found Karl with his mother; she put Mrs. Palmer's proposition in the politest and most agreeable form. Mrs. Hoffmann said nothing; she went on with her knitting, smiling to herself; but Karl was full of enthusiasm. He was sure the party would be every way charming; he greatly approved of the alteration in the day; a pleasure was always the greater, taken on the spur of the moment; he could answer for the willingness of all his friends to go a day earlier; the only people to whom it might be inconvenient were

the only people, he said, who with advantage might
be dropped from the party. He would undertake the
whole arrangement; and, as the weather was so
splendid, just hot enough, just bright enough, and
not dusty, after last night's rain, it was sure to be
a most charming and most successful excursion! It
was always a pleasure to him, he said, to go to
Neckarsteinach with people of taste and feeling—
especially with such people for the first time. So,
taking his hat, he said he would go instantly and
arrange everything, and, with Miss Palmer's permission, look in for five minutes in the evening, and
tell her what he had done.

The five minutes in the evening lengthened themselves to two hours. Karl had, of course, arranged
everything for the morrow most happily. He was in
the most buoyant spirits. Caroline played and sang
—Karl sang also, and Mrs. Palmer went into raptures
at finding a resemblance between his singing and
that of the favourite of her younger years, " the never-
to-be-excelled Braham." She quite forgot that she
had so lately been an invalid; she was charmed with
Karl, she was charmed with all the world; for the
Wilkinsons were coming; and many and many a
little anecdote she told, to convince her visiter that
the most munificent, the most princely nation under
the sun were the English, and that, of all the English,
the Wilkinsons were the most princely and munificent.

There was rain on the morning of the next day—
down-pouring rain, that from six till nine o'clock fell
upon the broad June leaves, with a sough that was
heard within doors. Many and many were the
anxious looks which both Karl and Caroline cast
from their windows, both up to the sky and down to
the earth; and, if it rained in this way all day, there
was certainly an end to the Neckarsteinach expedition;

and, once being put off, perhaps it might never be
made at all. How all-important does an afternoon's
excursion seem to the young! As to Mrs. Palmer,
she was in bed taking her breakfast very comfortably, and with great equanimity, and replied to her
daughter's anxiety, "Well, love, and even if it do
rain, I do not very much care. I have no great fancy
for this German party. I should have liked it much
better if we had gone alone, or, at all events, only the
Hoffmanns with us. I am only so far anxious about
the weather, as that it should be fine when the Wilkinsons arrive; the pleasantest places in the world
always look cheerless in wet weather; and as people
say it always rains at Heidelberg, I must confess, on
account of our friends' first impressions, I hope it
may be fine—at least on the day when they come."

It was much in the same spirit that good Mrs.
Hoffmann, above stairs, spoke of the rain to her son
during breakfast. "Never trouble yourself about the
weather, Karl," said she; "it will be fine most likely
long before noon; and even if it be not, it is not of
any great consequence. I never like altering days,
even of so unimportant a thing as a party of pleasure;
and I think it such a pity that poor Mrs. Von Holzhäuser cannot now go, so seldom as she has a day of
pleasure!"

Karl said he was sorry too, but he hoped it was
not so very great a disappointment to her.

"She took care that you should not see it," said
his mother, "for I am sure she thought much of this
little excursion—perhaps the only excursion that may
be offered her this summer—and she had made her
arrangements, you see, to be at liberty to-morrow.
She cannot alter, and then alter again with her pupils,
poor woman! It is a thousand pities that she must
be disappointed; but this all comes of making these

English people a party with us. I am very much vexed that they are going; and if it rain all day, it is of no great consequence!"

However, it did not rain all day. After nine o'clock the clouds grew thinner and thinner; glimpses of blue sky were seen, and faint shadows of the window-frames, cast slantingly along the floor, gave certain intimation that the sun was in the sky, and was very much disposed to shine. By eleven every cloud, and every trace of a cloud, was gone; and already, in the warm splendour of the advancing noon, the streets were dried, the trees also were dried, and only the bright green of the leaves, the bright hues of the flowers, and the deep colour of the earth, told that rain had fallen that morning. Every one of the party-expectant foreboded a wonderfully fine and pleasant afternoon; and good Mrs. Von Holzhäuser, the only elderly person who had looked forward to the excursion with anything like impatience—for to her a pleasure and a holiday came but seldom—rejoiced, for the sake of the young people, that the day would not prove a disappointment.

At two o'clock the party set out, every one apparently in the best of humour. There were three carriages—six worthy souls, young and old, in two of them—and four, the Palmers and the Hoffmanns, in the other.

" I have not the pleasure of knowing any of these good people," said Mrs. Palmer to Mrs. Hoffmann, as immediately they passed the Carl's Thor. The other two carriages relaxed their speed, in order that Mrs. Palmer might take the lead; and the gentlemen all, of course, bowed, and the ladies smiled with the utmost good humour.

" Many of them are familiar faces to me," said Caroline; " the two old ladies in the second carriage, the stout gentleman, the pretty girl in the pink bonnet, and the two young men in the last carriage that we passed, are all old acquaintance of mine. I have often seen them call on you, Mrs. Hoffmann," said she; "the old gentleman has such a noble, benevolent head, and the old ladies look so German, and so kind!"

"The old gentleman," said Karl, "is one of our best-known professors, in his particular branch; his name is familiar through Europe; one of the o.d lad'es is his wife; the other is the widow of a professor who, in his day, was not less renowned than the one I have just spoken of; the young girl in the pink bonnet is niece to the professor's widow : her mother is not living, and her father is a Herr Geheimerath, or privy councillor ; and, as he is a good deal at Carlsruhe, she spends much of her time with her aunt."

"Or rather," interrupted Mrs. Hoffmann, "the aunt spends much of her time with her; for there are no less than seven children, of which this young girl is the eldest: she is an excellent creature!"

"A most amiable girl," said Karl, with some enthusiasm, "and as well educated as she is amiable!"

Caroline wondered whether Karl Hoffmann had any particular reason for praising the young lady in the pink bonnet so warmly ; but as she could not ask, and he seemed not inclined to continue the subject, it dropped. "And the two young men in the same carriage," said she smiling; "I think they are friends of yours, Mr. Hoffmann; I think they are the same who were with you the evening you returned after your examination. How very German they look!—at least according to all my notions of young Germans; the long hair and the moustache is so becoming to some faces! I think one of your friends —he without the moustache—worthy to be a head of

Raphael's. Suppose his portrait the head of a young painter—suppose it the ideal head of an Athenian artist in the days of Pericles—how fine, how spiritual, we should say it was!"

"True," said Karl; "he is Von Rosenberg, one of my best friends. He is a noble-hearted fellow, of an old family, and is devoted to music. His history is a most interesting one. He has maintained himself ever since he was eighteen. He is a fine fellow every way."

"And the other," asked Caroline, "what is his name? for, in the first place, I am always curious about names. I have a little theory that names always resemble the persons who bear them—Von Rosenberg suits your friend admirably."

"His name is no way remarkable," said Karl; "it is Feldmann. He is my oldest friend; we were play-fellows together when boys; we were gymnasium scholars together; we have been fellow-students; what more was needed to make us friends? Feldmann is a very different character to Von Rosenberg; he is the most buoyant, happy being that ever lived; he is one born to be fortunate; all that he plans succeeds; all that he undertakes he carries through. The ship could not be wrecked in which Feldmann was! Poor Von Rosenberg! even as a boy, he knew many hard-ships and sorrows; he has already known grave dis-appointments; unfortunately he distrusts himself too much to be successful. If he had more confidence in himself, he would be one of the finest and most original of our modern composers. Poor fellow!" said Karl, in somewhat a lower voice, "whether he shall be the most happy or the most miserable of men, wavers now in, I fear, an uncertain balance. If the scale fall in his favour, I would venture to foretell for him the most splendid career; success,

which ruins so many men, would be the making of
him: if it fall against him, he is doubly unfortunate;
but come what will, he has one of the noblest hearts
that ever beat in a human bosom!"

"You interest me greatly for this young man,"
said she.

"He deserves it," replied Hoffmann; "and my
light-hearted Feldmann deserves it no less."

"You are fortunate," said she, "to have such
friends."

"Come, come, young people," said Mrs. Palmer,
"if you are to be talking sentiment all the time, what
will you see of the beauties of the country? and I
must warn you, Mr. Hoffmann, that if you indulge
Lina in sketching every character you know, you
may never have done. It is Lina's favourite topic of
conversation."

Caroline blushed, for she remembered sketching Mrs.
Wilkinson's character, at least in slight outline, as far
as she knew it, to Mrs. Hoffmann, and Mrs. Hoffmann
smiled likewise, for she remembered the same thing.

"In Heaven's name, where are we going?" screamed
Mrs. Palmer, clinging to the side of the carriage, with
a countenance of the utmost alarm, as the carriage,
having passed through the small city, or rather village
of Neckargemünd, made a sudden turn, and rapid
descent, to the ferry over the river. "Here I cannot,
will not go," screamed the terrified lady; "stop the
driver instantly, Mr. Hoffmann, for it is as much as
my life is worth to venture over this horrid place!"

With great difficulty the driver stopped his horses,
and drew aside to allow the other carriages to take
the advance in the ferry-boat.

"Is there no other way of getting to Neckarsteinach,
but over this frightful ferry?" asked she. She was
assured there was not for a carriage, but that there

was not the slightest danger. "I was once overset in a ferry-boat," said she; "I as near lost my life as possible; and I have never ventured over in one since, nor will I. Leave me behind if you will, but over it I will not go!"

"Let the carriage go first," said Mrs. Hoffmann, "and we will come over afterwards alone."

"No, no," still persisted the positive Mrs. Palmer, "I dare not venture."

"The other carriages are both safe over, dearest mamma; do let us venture," remonstrated Caroline. Karl also assured her that they should get over equally safe, but it was of no avail.

"Does Neckarsteinach lie on the river?" asked Caroline. She was answered that it did. "Would you not venture up in a boat?" inquired she, quite disconcerted by this unfortunate delay which her mother occasioned; "only think of all our charming boating-parties in England! Could we not get a boat?" asked she of Hoffmann.

"Nonsense! child," said her mother; "let me stay behind; nobody will miss me; the sight of this ferry has taken away all my desire to go. Is there no inn or house where I can stay till your return?"

Karl, with the utmost good temper, said 't was impossible that Mrs. Palmer could be left behind; that if she would go in a boat, he would immediately obtain one. Mrs. Hoffmann said that she should not wish to go in a boat so far; that perhaps one of the gentlemen in one of the other carriages would give her his place, and go with them in the boat; and that, for her part, she thought there was more danger in the boat than on the ferry. Caroline again remonstrated and persuaded, but to no purpose. Mrs. Palmer's fears, however foolish, were sincere; and at last, tired with her daughter's remonstrances, she grew

angry, and protested "that she was sorry to cause
annoyance to anybody; that she ought to have been
told of the ferry, for, in that case, she would not have
come!"

Karl had already ordered a boat; so, assisting his
mother to dismount, he accompanied her across the
ferry; and, whilst poor Caroline was hoping that their
companions did not think her mother altogether unreasonable and troublesome, and poor Mrs. Palmer, in a
self-deprecating tone of voice, was relating the adven-
ture on the ferry-boat, twenty years before, which
would haunt her, she said, with fears to the very day
of her death, Karl was making excuses, and offering
palliatives for Mrs. Palmer's childish apprehensions,
both to himself and all the rest of the party.

There was a deal of talking on the other side of the
river, and a long delay; at least, so it seemed both to
Caroline and her mother; but at length Karl returned
with not only one of his friends, but with both, and
with the pretty young lady in the pink bonnet also;
all three declaring, with the most perfect good humour,
that nothing in the world would charm them so much
as a row up the river; and, being received very graciously by Mrs. Palmer, and by Caroline with more
than her common cordiality—for she felt as if she had
a double duty of agreeableness and friendship to perform to everybody, after what had happened—all
took their seats in the boat, and the carriage being
ordered to await their return, they sailed pleasantly
up the river.

Mrs. Palmer, however, had been flurried and
excited; and, though she seemed in high spirits, there
was an under-current of vexation and ill-humour
ready at any untoward occurrence to break out: if
none of the others were aware of this, her daughter
was, and it kept her painfully watchful and anxious

But Hoffmann and his two friends, and the Herr Geheimrath's daughter, all seemed in such perfect good humour—so unannoyed by vexations, either past or to come—that she determined, if possible, to imitate their example, and enjoy the present moment at least.

How beautifully burst the scene upon them as they made the turn of the river at the foot of Dülsberg! There stood the castles in their varied degrees of antiquity, lying partly in broad light, and partly in deep shadow, crowning the rocks and bosomed in wood—the swallow's nest, the raven's castle, and the beautiful modernized castle of the Baron Von Dort, with its nameless ruins beyond! Caroline was delighted: it required, at that moment, no effort to forget all the late vexation; even Mrs. Hoffmann's countenance, glancing at her son a look of disgust and annoyance, as he helped her to dismount, the circumstance, perhaps, of all others, that had most disconcerted her—was forgotten. The party however, which was waiting for them at their place of landing, recalled her to the past, and convinced her, at the first glance, that the spirit of discontent was active among them. They were received almost without question or welcome; and, no sooner had they landed, than all turned and began immediately to ascend to the castles.

"I am sure they have been waiting a long time," said Caroline to her mother.

"Well, my dear, they need not have waited," was her mother's somewhat uncourteous reply.

"I fear you have waited long for us," said Caroline to Mrs. Hoffmann, in a very gentle and deprecating tone.

"Not quite an hour," replied she coolly; "the river is much farther than the road; parties do not commonly divide in this way!"

How reproved poor Caroline felt! she thought at the moment that it was unkind of Mrs. Hoffmann to

7

speak thus to her, who truly was not to blame; so, withdrawing again to her mother's side, they walked on in silence.

Karl seemed happy enough—so did his friends—so did the young lady in the pink bonnet. The old ladies, the old gentleman, and Mrs. Hoffmann, went on sometimes together, and sometimes singly, and sometimes they joined Caroline and her mother, and talked with them. How was it, Caroline questioned with herself, that she was unsatisfied and uneasy? that a feeling as of disappointment and repulse lay at the bottom of her heart? She thought the fault must be in herself; so she talked to every one, and laughed, and gathered wild berries and wild flowers, and sincerely admired the beauty of the place—the deep, secluded, old-world vallies that lie northward, the picturesqueness of every ruin—and listened with interest to every legend of the place which Karl Hoffmann or any one else of the party related. But oh, what a difference is there between trying to be pleased, and being pleased without an effort! She still was haunted by Mrs. Hoffmann's countenance, and by the few words she had spoken so coldly;—nay, even it seemed to her that Karl's gaiety was assumed—was greater than the occasion called for, and it really was only worn to set her at ease, or to hide his own vexation; and thus, spite of her sincerest wish to be happy, she remained ill at ease.

They all took coffee, and eat fruit at Neckarsteinach, and then prepared to return. Mrs. Palmer, and the same party who had attended her before, of course by water; but as, this time, they set off earlier than their friends, and went down with the current, they arrived at the ferry before them, and hoped to be in their carriage ready to drive along with them without any delay. But it was destined, altogether, to be a day of unlooked-for occurrences. From the ferry they intended to walk to the inn, but a great bustle in the street prevented their advance. A travelling carriage stood there with all the villagers crowded about it; evidently some disaster had occurred. The men-servants had dismounted, so had a gentleman from the inside; one of the four horses had suddenly died, and was being removed. A lady, the sole occupant of the carriage, was leaning back, evidently wishing to see nothing of what went forward, her face concealed by a large travelling-bonnet. Presently a carriage with other servants and luggage came up; it drew up for a moment, received orders from the gentleman, and from the lady also, and then drove on rapidly. There was some difficulty about another horse to supply the place of the one which was wanting, and so much bustle and confusion, that Karl, after several ineffectual efforts to gain attention, drew back to his party, thinking it better to wait till the strangers were satisfied and gone. Then suddenly, as if an idea had struck him, he turned to Caroline, and inquired the name of their English friends. "Wilkinson," was her reply.

"These, then, are they," said Karl; "the lady was addressed by that name."

"What is that you say?" eagerly inquired Mrs. Palmer, who caught at the idea at once, "the Wilkinsons here! Do inquire!"

Karl inquired; he was right.

"Take my card," said Mrs. Palmer, "and give it to the lady in the carriage; there is such a crowd, I cannot go myself!"

Hoffmann did as he was requested; and, the moment the lady read the card, she raised herself suddenly in the carriage, exclaiming, "Where—where is dear Mrs. Palmer?"

The crowd gave way before Mrs. Palmer and her

daughter; the carriage door was opened, the steps let down, and the two ladies, as if by instinct, hurried in, the hand of each grasped eagerly and warmly by the lady as they entered. The gentleman who had dismounted sprang in, the door was closed, the servants took their seats, and away all drove, leaving the dead horse on the side of the street, an object of curiosity to the people, now that the carriage was gone, and leaving Karl both vexed and surprised.

Mrs. Hoffmann, Karl, and his two friends, and the young lady in the pink bonnet, occupied the Palmers' carriage from Neckargemünd. Mrs. Hoffmann said very little on their homeward drive, nor did her son.

They needed not to have seen the Wilkinsons' arrival at Neckargemünd, to have assured them of the fact as they arrived at home. The carriage with luggage, from which the horses were taken, still stood at the door; servants were carrying in, and up stairs, large travelling-cases; there was a bustle and a stir, and an agitation through the whole of the house, that gave abundant evidence of the great people's arrival.

CHAPTER V.

KIND HEARTS.

THE next morning, Karl Hoffmann argued with his mother at the breakfast table, to prove—and that not quite against his own conviction—that the mere fact of Mrs. Palmer and her daughter returning from Neckargemünd with their friends, was neither uncourteous nor strange.

"It was but natural," said he; "I should have done the same thing myself most likely. Everybody prefers old friends to new ones."

"But if you treated your new friends with discourtesy —to say nothing of absolute rudeness, Karl—they would be greatly wanting in self-respect, if they ever gave you a second opportunity to do so; and thus my argument merely ends where it began—I have done with these English people."

Fortunately for Karl, his friend Von Rosenberg at that moment came in, to invite him to a long day's ramble into the hills. There was a gravity and earnestness in his countenance, which told Karl there was something of deep moment on his mind; Mrs. Hoffmann saw nothing of this, and, though Von Rosenberg declined to sit down, because Karl was immediately ready to accompany him, and both young men stood with their hats and their sticks in their hands, she insisted upon knowing, before they went, what was Von Rosenberg's opinion of the English ladies the last afternoon. He shrugged his shoulders; but a secret intelligence must have passed between him and his friend, for he immediately replied by taking Karl's view of the case, and argued for five minutes, even more strenuously than he himself had done, to prove that they had done not only what was reasonable, but what was right also.

"Away with you, for two wrong-headed philosophers!" exclaimed Mrs. Hoffmann, smiling in perfect good humour; "when I want special pleading, I'll come to you; but when I want only the plain common sense of a question, I'll reason for myself."

The young men smiled, bowed, and withdrew; and she, with a smile still on her lips—for she was thinking with affection on her son and his friend—busied herself in putting aside the breakfast things. Von Rosenberg linked his arm into Karl's the moment they were out of the door, and both walked on slowly, as if falling at once into deep and confidential communing, quite unaware of the observation of Caroline Palmer, who was in the balcony above watering her flowers, which, in the bustle and excitement of the evening before, had been quite forgotten.

The afternoon's excursion had been altogether unsatisfactory to her; she was sure that her mother's needless apprehensions would appear childish, if not ridiculous, to their German friends; and then, to crown all, that hurrying away at last, without apology or explanation, with their English friends, though in itself perhaps neither unnatural nor blameable, still, occurring on the heels of the other cause of dissatisfaction, was greatly to be regretted. Caroline had wept the last night in her own chamber, for mortification; but what good did that do? it convinced no kind German heart whatever, how unwilling she must ever be to displease or to slight them; so she dried her tears, and had awoke this morning with some unpleasant consciousness still remaining, but with a half-hope that she could soon prove to the Hoffmanns that she was as kindly disposed to them as ever. She determined, therefore, as soon as possible after breakfast, to make a call on the mother; with the anxious hope, however, that Karl might be present, for she not only knew him much more reasonable, much more unprejudiced than his mother, but she had long since seen also that her wishes were almost a law with him— which was gratifying to her vanity and self-love, if not to any deeper and nobler sentiment. She made sure, therefore, that with a little skill on her part, she would still maintain this intimacy, which had hitherto been not only so agreeable, but so improving to her.

It was therefore with no slight regret, if not mortification, that she saw him go out thus early with his friend, and in that peculiarly confidential manner, too!—not as they commonly did, looking gaily about them, as if with unburdened hearts, but with linked arms, and grave, earnest countenances. It seemed at once to her, as if they were talking on unpleasant subjects, and, filled as her mind was with but one unpleasant subject, it is no wonder that she troubled herself with the fear that their conference might be on that. She wished she had not seen them thus go out; she was ashamed to confess to herself, that this little circumstance would annoy her all the day; add to which, she had now no longer confidence as to the effect of her call on Mrs. Hoffmann. Poor Caroline! about an hour afterwards she saw Mrs. Hoffmann also go out; so she went up stairs, and made a call in her absence, taking with her a beautiful bouquet, which she gave to the little Bena, with strict injunctions to put it in water, and set it on Mrs. Hoffmann's table, and to give her love, and say that she had called to inquire after Mrs. Hoffmann's health, and that she was extremely sorry not to find her in, as she had a great deal to say to her. Bena promised to remember every word, and to put the flowers in a very pretty glass of water; and, thinking to herself, that the " English Fräulein" was a great deal lovelier even than these lovely flowers, she watched her down the stairs, and then went to perform her promise.

Karl Hoffmann and his friend had indeed a long and very deep communing that morning, on a very important and interesting topic. On they went farther and farther among the wooded hills, till they came to the lonely village of Wilhelm Fells, whence, after making, in the humble wirthshaus there, a most rustic dinner, they again walked home, taking less heed that day than they had ever done before, to the singularly wild and beautiful ramble they had chosen.

Although Caroline Palmer had feared—perhaps not unnaturally—that she and her mother might make part, if not the whole, of this day's conversation between the two friends, it is not for us to say whether she would have been gratified or displeased had the truth been made known to her, that only very incidentally, through that day, were their names mentioned by them. It was another name that was most on their lips, and who was the sole cause of this day's ramble and this confidential communing—it was the name of the pretty young lady in the pink bonnet, the Herr Geheimerath, or privy councillor's daughter, the gentle and truehearted Pauline Damian.

The handsome English carriage, looking bright and clean, as if new, even after its journey out of Italy, with four horses and two attendants seated on the box, in livery somewhat too showy for good taste, having taken Mrs. Wilkinson, Arthur Burnett, and the two Palmers for a morning-drive to Weinheim, was dashing over the bridge of the Neckar at a rate which terrified the quiet citizens, about four o'clock in the afternoon, as Karl and his friend, still walking arm in arm, were leisurely returning home from their ramble. Caroline's heart suddenly beat quicker, with a thrill of pleasure. The young men bowed, but with countenances of the utmost gravity.

" How ridiculously solemn a German looks when he bows to you!" exclaimed Mrs. Wilkinson, laughing.

Arthur Burnett turned round to Caroline, and bowed à la German.

" That is exactly the face of that young Hoffmann!" said Mrs. Palmer; " I shall absolutely be afraid of your Mr. Burnett!" added she.

" Oh, he is a terrible mimic," said Mrs. Wilkinson. "Arthur, you must give us the family of the Jenkinses after dinner—it is so beautifully absurd! We saw it ourselves—they were Birmingham tradespeople—a whole family at Florence, just arrived, who could speak a word neither of French nor Italian!"

Caroline wondered with herself whether Karl Hoffmann would appear to advantage among her English
friends: she feared not; he had seen so much less of
the world, and was naturally so much less assuming.

Karl's ramble with his friend that day ended in his
spending the evening with him in the house of the
Geheimerath, who, however, was absent in Carlsruhe.
Still the good aunt was at home; and there was
Pauline, looking so kind and so happy; and all the
six brothers and sisters—a family of love—so good-
tempered, and healthy, and amiable. Von Rosenberg
had sent his violoncello there that afternoon, and Pauline
now accompanied him on the piano. Karl played at
chess with the second sister, and then at the favourite
game of the-bell-and hammer with the younger children,
while the good aunt sate on the sofa knitting, like all
German women entering into everybody's pleasure, and
looking the very image of universal benevolence.

After the younger children were gone to bed, and
Von Rosenberg and Pauline were practising together a
new piece of music, the aunt invited Karl to a seat beside
her on the sofa, for a little confidential conversation; the
sum and substance of which was, that although she
had sanctioned the young people's being together that
evening, because she had reason to believe that her
brother had the highest esteem for Von Rosenberg, and
had, all the winter, allowed him the most friendly intercourse with the family, and, she did not doubt, would
put no impediment in the way of his and Pauline's
wishes, yet still, after this evening, until her brother
had been made acquainted with what had taken place,
she would never again allow Von Rosenberg to enter
the house.

Karl said he would go with his friend the very next
day to Carlsruhe; the old lady expressed herself quite
satisfied, and then rolled up her knitting; and, order-

ing the maid to bring in supper, busied herself in
preparing the table for the meal. Karl looked on
his friend's countenance that evening, beaming as it
was with affectionate happiness, and he thought, if
Caroline Palmer could but have seen it then, how
much more would she have been struck with its
spirituality, and high tone of beauty.

The Herr Geheimerath, or Privy Councillor Damian,
was sitting the next afternoon in his schlaf-rock, or
morning-coat and slippers, smoking from a very long
and handsome pipe, in the little room which he called
his study, in his small lodgings at Carlsruhe.   There
was a great quantity of newspapers lying on the table
before him, a great many bundles of written papers,
and books, in the utmost disorder, neither in modern
nor in handsome bindings, occupied a set of shelves
on one side of the room; on the opposite side, a great
many pipes, of every variety of size and fashion, were
displayed, in the midst of which, however, hung a
large gilt-framed and glazed engraved portrait of the
present Grand Duke of Baden, evidently the most
esteemed ornament of the room; a smoking-cap,
however, hung upon the hook which sustained the
picture, from which, perhaps, no very false inference
might be drawn, that with the Geheimerath, loyalty
and love of tobacco were about equally strong passions.

Altogether the room had a very slovenly and dis-
orderly appearance; the floor, of course, was un-
carpeted, but it was, besides this, not remarkably
clean; the chairs had that day been but very partially
dusted, and the muslin curtains of the three large
windows might, with some advantage, have been
washed at least a month before. But the worthy
occupant of the room troubled himself about none of
these things. He knew that the excellent grand
duke not only had great esteem for his judgment and

abilities, but respected him as a man; and in his own heart and conscience he was at ease with himself; so he took no thought either about his dingy curtains or his dirty chairs; and, so far as concerned either his pride or his comfort, his rooms might have been the best in the palace itself. On this particular afternoon, having dined as usual at one o'clock, although he had taken up the *Algemeine Zeitung*, as was his custom, to read it, it remained quietly on his knee unread; and, seated in his old cushioned chair, he gave himself up to the pleasure of that very long and very handsome pipe. Perhaps the tobacco that afternoon was particularly good, for he had just opened a new packet of superfine cnaster; most likely it was so, for he thought with himself he never had smoked so excellent a pipe—never one which had relished so much, and he was meditating with himself whether he should not re-fill his pipe and smoke a second, when a knock at his door announced an interruption, and, in answer to his permission to enter, Von Rosenberg presented himself. The kind-hearted old man bade him cordially welcome, internally rejoicing over himself, that now he could smoke a second pipe in company with his visiter. But the visiter declined, although the handsomest pipe from the collection on the wall was offered him, and after having been invited to test the new-opened cnaster by scent.

"Yes, yes," said the good Geheimerath, laughing, "young men, now-a-days, cannot smoke out of a schlaf-rock; and there is some reason in it. Now, if I were at home I could accommodate you in this respect; and even here, until yesterday, I had two, but I unfortunately tore one of them last week on the door handle; it was but an old one, to be sure, but I sent it away to a poor sick fellow yesterday, or it might have done to wear on an occasion, or to save a better coat."

We need not give the precise words in which Von Rosenberg made known to the Geheimerath the object of his visit. The Herr Geheimerath smoked his fresh pipe, and said so very little, that poor Von Rosenberg remained half an hour afterwards in a most wretched. state of uncertainty. He had not another word to say; and he thought he never had spoken so ill, never had looked so foolish in all his life before; still the Geheimerath smoked on, and said nothing. Every minute seemed five; the old gentleman took up the *Algemeine Zeitung*, and seemed as if he were going to read it through; and then, without laying down the paper, and with the pipe between his lips, and looking over his spectacles, inquired if Von Rosenberg had come to Carlsruhe alone? He replied that Karl Hoffmann was with him.

" You can both come and eat some supper with me, at eight o'clock," said the Herr Geheimerath; " I have some good Johannisberg, and then we can talk over this foolish affair of yours together."

" Your father and I were each other's best friend at the University of Berlin," said the kind old man to Von Rosenberg, as they and Hoffmann sat together over the supper-table, each with a sparkling glass of that noble Rhine wine in their hands; " let us drink to his memory !" said he, winking his eyelids close, and giving a very peculiar expression to his countenance, so as to prevent a tear from falling. " To the memory of Ludwig Von Rosenberg, the truest and kindest friend that ever man had !"

The three glasses were filled to the brim, and, being all angestossen, or clinked together, were emptied at a draught. The old man set his glass down with a violence that shivered it to pieces. " It is right," said he; " it shall never be polluted by being drank **from** to a less worthy man's memory !" and then, filling another glass, he drank it in silence to his own thoughts.

"And so your uncle is married?" said he, turning abruptly to Von Rosenberg.

"He has been married," replied he, "for many years."

"There is no hope of inheritance from him, then?' said the other.

"None whatever," replied he.

"And," said the Geheimerath—"for we may as well come to plain speaking at first—your father died poor."

Von Rosenberg felt as if upon the rack, but he replied, with apparent coolness, that his father had left but very little property behind him. "He died suddenly," said he; "a state letter, containing a much higher appointment, arrived the very day after his death. He left five children, of whom I was the eldest."

"I know, I know," interrupted the Geheimerath, giving him his hand; "I know what you have already done; nor can I praise you higher than in saying that you are a worthy son of Ludwig Von Rosenberg. But you studied political economy in Tübingen, and passed your examination most creditably; why abandon this, your true vocation?"

"I shrunk," replied the young man, with the most perfect candour, "from the prospect which that vocation presented me in life. To vegetate in a small city, where my sole associates must be peasants; where the only two educated, beside myself—the doctor, and the pastor—had sunk down into little better than peasants themselves. I shrunk from this, perhaps the more especially, because I have laid out for myself a very different, and, as it seemed to me, a far nobler course in life."

"As a composer of music?" said the Geheimerath.

"The same," replied Von Rosenberg.

"All very well," said the other, cooly, "did I not know that many an imaginative young man runs away from duty, after anything that looks, for the time, more alluring, and thus brings ruin on himself and friends."

"Only let me be assured," said Von Rosenberg, with an earnestness that made his countenance almost colourless, "that the one dear wish of my heart may be accomplished, and I will then soon prove that I have been led by no ignis-fatuus! Try for years, if you will," continued he, seeing that the other remained silent; "put me to what test you will, only do not take from me hope!"

The Geheimerath smiled, and then looked very grave.

"Were not * * * and * * * poor?" continued Von Rosenberg, "and where, throughout the whole world now, are there more honourable names?"

"And were not many of the most celebrated men of the present day," remarked Hoffmann, "in every department of science and philosophy, poor also?— there, for instance, is the Herr Geheimerath's own friend."

"It is a fine school, that same much dreaded poverty," replied the Geheimerath, "both morally and intellectually, for the mind that is strong enough to overcome it; but I am not objecting to your want of money my dear young friend," said he, most kindly, and laying his hand on Von Rosenberg's arm, but I want to be assured yet that you have sufficient original power in music to make it prudent to abandon every other prospect in life for it."

"I have given as yet but little evidence of my power," said Von Rosenberg, overcoming an emotion which for the instant filled his eyes with tears, but I have hitherto struggled only with difficulties—with uncertainties. Some minds are stimulated by difficulty and impediment; the very existence of opposition creates the power to overcome it; these are minds of the highest order—mine is of a different character; the prospect of success—the belief in the ultimate accomplishment of a hope—I care not how remote that accomplishment lies—has ever enabled me to succeed. As I have been candid in confessing my weakness," added he, " believe me also when I tell you in what my strength lies. I have courage for every hardship; I have perseverance for every difficulty; but I must have hope! Have confidence in me, my friend, my father's friend," said he, his noble countenance kindling with a light as of inspiration, "and neither you nor Pauline shall be disappointed. I know how great is the reward for which I am asking, but I know also, that in the certain prospect of this reward, I am able to deserve it. Pauline loves me," added he, with a proud earnestness; " this surely might have been stimulus enough—why have I sought for more?"

" Because," said the Geheimerath, " Ludwig Von Rosenberg's son could not have done less. Thou hast done right, and thou shalt have thy wish! Give me thy hand, son of my old friend, and may God Almighty bless thee!"

Their hands were fast locked together; the Geheimerath again winked his eyes, and wrinkled his face into a very comical expression; and poor Von Rosenberg, bowing his head to the table, wept vehemently.

" Come, come," said the old man, " this is only fit for women and children; fill thy glass, Karl Hoffmann, and fill Von Rosenberg's also." Von Rosenberg could not speak; he rose from the table and went to the window, from which, for the next five minutes, he looked out, or seemed to look out, into the summer moonlight; but he that while had vowed himself to the highest efforts of his art—had registered a vow in heaven, to spend all the fervour of his soul in becoming worthy of that good old man's daughter.

The Geheimerath Damian returned with the two young men to Heidelberg. Pauline knew instantly, when the carriage stopped at the door that Sunday afternoon, bringing her father so unexpectedly back, that the lover's journey had been a happy one, and, kissing him with the warmest affection and gratitude, she bade him kindly welcome.

It was soon noised abroad through all the little city, that the fair Pauline Damian was the betrothed bride of Von Rosenberg. The bride and bridegroom, according to custom, made calls on all their acquaintance, and received congratulations.

"I must return in two days to Carlsruhe," said the Geheimerath, after he had been about a week with his family; "let us have all our friends invited for to-morrow evening, that I may drink with them to the happiness of the young people, and then Von Rosenberg must prepare for his journey."

How busy the good aunt was all that day, and what invitations were sent out, which everybody accepted!

It would indeed have reconciled a misanthrope to the human race, to have taken supper that next night at the Herr Geheimerath Damian's. There was such cordiality, such unceremonious politeness, such universal good understanding among them all; such glowing friendships among the young, such proved friendships among the old—not to speak about the good eating and drinking, nor the merry conversation, the flashes of wit, nor the deep philosophy! It was no wonder that, when they rosé to depart, they were amazed to

find it past midnight. Although it was late when the
company left the Geheimerath's door, Von Rosenberg
and his friend did not separate.

Von Rosenberg opened all his plans of life to his
friend. He opened to him his whole soul, even as he
had never before done, for he could now look his
doubts and despondencies in the face, and think them
chimeras; and all his aspirings and dreams of distinc-
tion, which before had seemed so baseless and futile,
appeared now only like the foreshadowings of his
future celebrity.

His mind was of a devotional cast, and his
favourite, and hitherto his most successful music, had
been of a religious character. When a boy, he had
strolled over many parts of Catholic Germany, from
cathedral to cathedral, from convent to convent,
delighting himself with, and in some degree studying,
the music of processions, of dirges, and masses. His
determination now was to begin afresh the same study
in the same way; to place himself in the very sanc-
tuaries of this holy and peculiar music, and give
expression to the emotions of his own soul to cathedral organs, and the chanting of lonely monks. He
would take, he said, his knapsack on his back, and
travel, even like a common handwerksbursche, or wan-
dering journeyman, from city to city, through Germany,
France, and Italy, and create himself a name in this
glorious yet unhacknied path of music.

Karl strengthened his determination, sympathised
with him in all his glowing hopes, and so they parted—
Karl to spend the night partly in dreams of his friend,
and partly in dreams, not sleeping but waking, which
nearly concerned himself, but in which the reader, as
yet, has nothing to do; and Von Rosenberg to compose—an earnest of his future honour—a magnificent
piece of music, which very soon thrilled through and

through the music-loving heart of Germany, and which almost immediately established his name as one of her most favourite modern composers.

CHAPTER VI.

SEEKING AFTER AMUSEMENT.

More than a week passed, and the Palmers and the Hoffmanns saw nothing of each other. By degrees the vexatious memory of the afternoon at Neckarsteinach had faded away from Caroline's mind; the time for apologies and explanations was gone by; and it seemed to her as if she had magnified mere trifles into vast importance. Besides this, she began to fancy that she, perhaps, had given to these new German acquaintance an influence and a control, as it were, over her feelings and her conduct, which was very absurd. She was always, she said, so guided by her imagination; she had invested all quiet, old-fashioned Germans, ever since she had known that good Mrs. Von Völining, with such a panoply of virtues; and, really after all—turning again to the Neckarsteinach afternoon—Mrs. Hoffmann had been uncourteous, and even unjust to her. Then there was something in the dashing, off-hand, uncounting-of-cost, and decided manner and style of the new English associates, which was captivating. Her reason told her, that here again her imagination was caught, and that there was far more danger in her admiring these new characteristics, than by imagining even that every social virtue was German. She was in an uncomfortable state of indecision between two opinions, and she began most earnestly to wish she could bring not national, but individual character, side by side, as it were into close comparison, and discover the truth.

Thus she persuaded herself that it was merely for the solution of a moral problem, that one day, when wearied both by Arthur Burnett's mimicry and flattery, she began sincerely to wish that Karl Hoffmann, with his love of music, and his quiet good sense, would come down to spend the evening with them, as he used so often to do before the Wilkinsons came; and,.full of this idea, she determined at once to go and call upon his mother.

Karl had his hat in his hand when she entered the room, but he immediately laid it down, and took a seat. Both she and Mrs. Hoffmann seemed constrained; the old lady evidently was not cordial, and Caroline at once determined to spare no pains to win her back into perfect friendship. Mrs. Hoffmann, on her side, who, for the last ten days, had rejoiced in the cessation of all intercourse, was acting now on that mode of conduct she had avowed to her son— she would no longer have any intimacy with these English people. Caroline's wish to please made her really pleasing; but the mother had made up her mind not to be won, and, though she smiled almost graciously, she was as cool as possible in her manner. Karl had never appeared so friendly, so agreeable before, for he, knowing his mother's true sentiments, perhaps thought it needful to show civility for them both.

At length Caroline rose to depart, when Karl, taking up a little roll of music which he had laid down with his hat, said that he was intending to have left it at her door when he passed; that Von Rosenberg had copied it out for her at his request. It was, he said, his friend's last composition, and had been composed under the happiest circumstances, and he doubted not but she would be delighted with it.

Caroline smiled her grateful thanks, and glanced at the title—The Betrothal.

"Indeed!" exclaimed she, the joyful truth at once flashing to her mind, "then your friend is happy! Allow me to say how much, how sincerely I rejoice!" Karl took a small card from a number of others which were wedged round the looking-glass frame, and presented it to her. It was small, with a gold border, and elegantly engraved, "Ludwig Max Von Rosenberg—Pauline Isabelle Marie Damian, verlobt September 12, 183—."

"Ah!" exclaimed she, "the lovely girl who went with us to Neckarsteinach! I am delighted! Poor Mr. Von Rosenberg!"

"He does not need any one's pity," said Mr. Hoffmann.

"I did not mean to pity him," replied Caroline, "but, from my soul, I sympathise in his happiness. Congratulations, of course, are proper on such events. I can have no opportunity of offering mine either to him or her; let me, therefore, congratulate you as his friend; and," added she, though somewhat in a lower voice, "this joyful event makes something you said the other day perfectly intelligible. I am, indeed, delighted;" and, glancing again at the card, with eyes full of kindness and pleasure, she laid it upon the table.

"Von Rosenberg," said Karl, "leaves Heidelberg almost immediately—perhaps not to return for years."

"That is strange!" replied Caroline.

"He will not marry," said Karl, "till he has acquired for himself reputation, if not fortune. He sets out now on his year or years of learning. I also shall do the same," added he. "We shall set off like two handwerksburschen, or travelling journeymen, with knapsacks on our backs."

"With a respectable show of old shoes and boots strapped on the outside," said Caroline, laughing, upon whose mind, however, this intimation of Karl's early departure came like a sudden cloud, "and with a little pair of wheels on which to draw your knap-sacks when you are weary. We shall have you begging at our carriage steps—'A few kreutzers—be so good—to pay for our night's lodgings!'"

"Certainly," said Karl.

"But," continued Caroline, "your friend, with his beautiful hair, and glorious countenance, will get far more kreutzers than you. One always bestows one's money among the handsome beggars."

"But," replied Karl, "I shall be the bold hand-werksbursche, Von Rosenberg will sit twirling his stick on the bench by the road-side, and I shall beg."

"And are they really going?" asked Caroline, turning to Mrs. Hoffmann.

"Yes," replied she, "as soon as their things are ready."

"I always think," said Caroline, trying to look unconcerned, "a handwerksbursche has a pleasant life of it while the fine weather lasts; but, methinks you are setting off somewhat late in the season. No doubt, however, you'll get hired to some master, in a cheerful city, for the winter."

"Certainly," returned Karl, with the most imper-turbable gravity.

The seven rooms which Mrs. Palmer had hired for her friends, were found to be too few for them, and some of the servants had to be lodged out. Caroline's bed-room, which, unfortunately for her, adjoined that of Mrs. Wilkinson, was begged from her for that lady's French maid, and Caroline was removed into a little inconvenient chamber beyond their own sitting-room; but anything and everything must be done to accommodate and satisfy dear Mrs. Wilkinson.

"I am sorry, dearest Caroline," said that lady, "to inconvenience you, but I cannot do without Mademoiselle Rosalie close at hand."

"We are all like one family," said Mrs. Palmer; "I am sure Lina's greatest pleasure is to oblige you."

Caroline said that she found the change rather a convenience, as she thus could rise early in a morning to practise, without passing through her mother's chamber, as she had hitherto done, and thus disturbing her. Before long another alteration was proposed. Mrs. Palmer's sitting-room—that pleasant room that opened into the balcony, and that Caroline, she hardly knew why, liked so very much—was found to be nearer to Mrs. Wilkinson's kitchen than the one which had been first fixed upon for her dining-room, so Mrs. Palmer was solicited to allow it to become the dining-room; "because," said Mrs. Wilkinson, "you must always dine with us. It is a miserable way sending out for your dinner—nothing hot nor as it should be; and my cook is quite an artist. We must all dine together. My sitting-room is yours, and only very little further from your bed-rooms; Lina's harp shall be carried in; and, now I have hired the new tables, and those handsome rugs, it looks quite English. I shall, however, have still some brackets put in the walls, and arrange on them, and about the room, some of those vases, and things I brought from Italy—for I hate these unfurnished German apartments; and, when Lina and her harp are in it, it will look quite charming. And do you know, Mrs. Palmer," said she, in a very confidential tone, "Arthur says that Lina is the most graceful English girl he ever saw. She reminds us both of Lady Charlotte Hay, that I told you everybody in Florence was in love with—only I think, and so he thinks, that Lina is still handsomer."

Mrs. Palmer after this could say nothing against giving up the dining-room. "And as to your maid," continued the munificent Mrs. Wilkinson, " she must always dine with our servants; and you must let Rosalie give her a lesson or two in hair-dressing; she has a very nice notion, but she will be the better for Rosalie's teaching."

In a fortnight's time, therefore, a very considerable change had taken place in Mrs. Palmer's little establishment. Caroline passed most of her time in Mrs. Wilkinson's sitting-room; but it was vain attempting to get up early now to practise, for Arthur Burnett also rose early in a morning to train his New-foundland dog, which he always did in the sitting-room; and, now that their own room was given up for dining, it was no longer sacred from the entrance of the Wilkinsons' servants, who soon found it convenient to set out Mr. Arthur's breakfast there; or it had to be prepared for an early luncheon; or to be cleaned; or a missing spoon or fork had to be searched for: there was no longer any privacy in it. Caroline thought to herself, that she was, after all, very much incommoded, but she took it all patiently; and Mrs. Palmer, who never left her bed-room till eleven o'clock, and therefore was no way annoyed, and who only remarked, if her daughter chanced to complain, "Oh, love, I am sure you are glad to oblige Mrs. Wilkinson!" and who infinitely preferred the better furnished sitting-room, and better furnished table of her friend, therefore found herself very happy.

The large case containing the beautiful casts and marbles which had been brought from Italy, sorely to their damage, had been unpacked, and such as were thought most appropriate and ornamental were taken out, " that some marks of mind," said Mrs. Wilkinson, " might be visible in these inelegant German rooms. Two antiques of great beauty were placed upon the public staircase, in two large niches, which seemed very invitingly to want filling; a pair of richly-wrought vases were placed upon the brackets in the sitting-room; a Laocoon stood upon a little side-table which was hired for the purpose; while a Hebe and a Magdalen of Canova stood upon black marble pedestals; and various little Cupids throwing balls, selecting arrows, and engaged in other such pastimes, with intaglios of great beauty, vases of terra-cotta, and a variety of curiosities from Pompeii, ornamented what-nots, and tables, were arranged in elegant disorder, according to the most approved English mode.

"It is hardly worth while to have been at all this trouble for so short a stay, perhaps," said Mrs. Wilkinson; "but as Caroline wished to see them, and one had need try to find some amusement in this dull place, it is of no consequence. We can have a man from Mannheim to pack them all again." So everything was spread abroad and examined, and such as were not wanted were given to Mademoiselle Rosalie and Arthur Burnett's valet, to put back into the case again.

Caroline one morning was standing with a small vase in her hand, studying, with great attention, its beautiful design, whilst her mother and Mrs. Wilkinson were reclining on the sofas. "Well, I must confess," said the latter lady, with a most expressive yawn, "that I am greatly disappointed in this Heidelberg. The castle is only an unshapely mass of red stone, and walls looking patchy with old whitewash." Caroline turned round suddenly, and stood with the vase still in her hand. "Yes, you may look, Lina," said she, "but I have seen all the splendid ruins in Italy, and all those in England; and, let Mrs.

Jameson say what she will, the Coliseum, even without moonlight, is infinitely before this castle; nay, even in my mind, Bolton Abbey, or Fintun or Fountains, standing, as they do, in their paradisaical vales, and bosomed in their magnificent trees, are, any one of them—not so large, I grant—but more picturesque and beautiful."

" I have only seen Bolton Abbey," said Caroline, setting down the vase; " but eh! it seems like treason to compare it even with this glorious castle—this mass of palaces—any one of which, nay even a single tower of which, would be a splendid ruin. Then look at its stupendous walls, as if built by Titans—not crumbled away by time, but rent and shattered by violence—every corner tower gone, and the abrupt, sharp angles of broken walls left like rocks torn asunder by earthquakes! Look at that Gesprengte Thurm, does it not remind one of the wars of giants? Look again at that magnificent palace of Otto Heinrich, with its arabesques and graceful sculptures, any one figure of which is worthy to be by a pupil of Raphael!"

" You are so enthusiastic," said Mrs. Wilkinson laughing; " you look so much at the detail of a thing —think so much of its poetry—I take a thing in its whole; and, I say again, that tourists make a great riot about nothing, when they say so much about Heidelberg! What say you, Mrs. Palmer?"

" I take a middle course," said that politic lady

" Then, as to the mountains," continued Mrs. Wilkinson ; " good Heavens! to call them mountains! —round-backed hills, and nothing else! Go to Switzerland for mountains, or to the Apennines, nay, even to our own Wales or Cumberland!"

" I have seen neither the Alps nor the Apennines," said Caroline, " but I know perfectly almost every sheep-track up Skiddaw and Helvellyn, Cader Idris and

Snowdon—but I should never think of comparing them with these hills. These dear, round-backed green hills —for we will not call them mountains—suit the character of this scenery, with its vineyards and scattered villages, its deep old-world valleys, where children herd goats, and women spread out the linen which they have spun in the winter to bleach, and where a couple of yoked cows slowly drag along the old-fashioned waggon, and everything seems so stil. and so simple, so full of that spirit of quiet and contentment, which has so entirely left the home of the English poor. Oh, I love this old-fashioned primitive land of Germany!''

"I always told you you were German-mad!" said her mother.

"Take care Arthur does not hear you talk in this strain," said Mrs. Wilkinson, "or you will never hear the last of it."

Caroline took up the little vase again, and thought that if Arthur Burnett ridiculed her, she should very much dislike him.

"But to return to what I was saying," said Mrs. Wilkinson, "I do think Heidelberg prodigiously stupid:—no concerts—no promenades—no public rooms—no opera! What, in the world, is there? Are there no people worth knowing?"

"I have some letters of introduction," said Mrs. Palmer, "but they are all to professors."

"Heaven defend me from professors!" exclaimed Mrs. Wilkinson; "they know nothing but their own particular branch of science or philosophy, and their wives know nothing but household economy. I once was betrayed into making the acquaintance of a professor at Berlin; we were invited there to supper, and our supper consisted of two sorts of sausages, two sorts of salad, and two sorts of wine, each sour as vinegar! I must get Arthur to read you the epigram

he wrote on that memorable supper!" and again
Mrs. Wilkinson yawned. "But come, Lina," said
she, raising herself up on the sofa, "I was so sleepy
last night, that I confess I heard nòt a single note of
what you played. I am tired even now, but I want
to hear the new piano; so sit down, and I promise
you not to sleep again."

Caroline sate down to the grand piano which had
been hired from Mannheim, and began to play the
piece which Karl Hoffmann had given her.

"Oh, but this is really superb! This is most splendid music!" said Mrs. Wilkinson—who had naturally
a fine taste in music—rising from the sofa when Caroline had finished; "whose is it, dear?"

Caroline's eyes were full of tears. There was
something in that music which touched her deeply.
She thought of the beautiful head and countenance of
its composer—of his early misfortunes—his timid,
uncertain love—the influence, for happiness or misery,
which that love would have upon his life—all which
Karl Hoffmann had told her, and which this music
spoke so plainly; and then the sudden change in its
tone and spirit—the lover was accepted! a colouring
like the morning was cast over everything—the earth,
the sky, man and woman, the present and the future—
all was bright, all was full of a new glory!—then
there was a change, and all breathed of domestic
peace, and confidence, and love; the accepted bridegroom was received into the bosom of a new family;
new chains of affection were linked about him; there
was a holy calm over everything, as if a father's blessing, and a mother's tears, and loving angels in heaven,
had hallowed it! Then followed a burst like that of
joyful hearts speaking aloud—as of the laughter of
young brothers and sisters, the clinking of glasses,
the drinking to the happiness of the betrothed: a

low symphony closed it—the friends were gone; the bride and the bridegroom had parted, and blessed dreams, like the fluttering of angels' wings, gathered round the pillow of each.   It was more intelligible than words to Caroline, and, burying her face, in her hands, she wept.

"It is glorious music!" said Mrs. Wilkinson, taking it from the instrument; "but this is manuscript!"

Caroline wiped her eyes. "I am very foolish," she said, "but this music affects me strangely.   It was composed only a few days ago by one of Mr. Hoffmann's friends, on his own betrothal, I believe."

"He is quite a genius!" said Mrs. Wilkinson; "we must know him; he can, perhaps, help to amuse us—who is he?"

"A Mr. Von Rosenberg," replied Caroline; "you remember him, mamma, with the long, beautiful hair; he went with us in the boat to Neckarsteinach.   He has since then been betrothed to Miss Damian—that pretty girl in the pink bonnet.   He calls this wonderful music, very properly, The Betrothal.' Its deep sentiment, its truthful domestic character, its holy, affectionate spirit, make it perfectly glorious," said she.

"I should think you might ask Mr. Hoffmann to bring him some evening," said Mrs. Palmer; "and, now I think of it—how long it is since that young man was here!—he sings admirably."

"Come, come!" said Mrs. Wilkinson, looking quite animated, "with a composer like this—what's his name?—Von Rosentein—your singing Mr. Hoffmann, yourself, Lina, and your singing-mistress, I declare we might get up a little concert.   Unfortunately Arthur cares nothing for music—but I really must manage it; that dining-room of yours, Lina, we might fit up so sweetly, with an awning over the balcony.   We must do it!"

" Will you call with me on Mrs. Hoffmann?" said Caroline, to Mrs. Wilkinson; " you know here the strangers must make the first advance."

" But why need to call in Mrs. Hoffmann at all? we only want the son," replied Mrs. Wilkinson.

" I don't exactly know," replied she, " but he seems to have such respect and reverence for his mother—I think it is rather characteristic of a German —that, as we have had the misfortune to offend her, we must, in the first place, get her into good humour, and then the son will be at our service." She then related what had happened at Neckarsteinach. " You, see," said Mrs. Palmer, " I was so taken by surprise —I had expected you so long and so earnestly, that at the moment I forgot all about those people, and I am not sure that I either made apology or excuse for leaving them."

" We can soon get over that little difficulty," said Mrs. Wilkinson; " I never yet met with foreigners who were not flattered by the civilities of the rich English; and besides that, I am never without a little ' soft sawder,' as Slam Slick says."

" Sam Slick has clipped many of my angels' wings," said Caroline laughing. " I used so happily to believe all the fine things people said either to me or to mamma, till I read Sam Slick."

" She uses too much soft sawder herself, not to know what is soft sawder in other people's mouths," said Mrs. Wilkinson to Caroline's mother. " Is not that true?"

" I never flatter," said Caroline, eagerly.

" Then I am sure, Lina," returned her mother, " you have no business to court this Mrs. Hoffmann, for she is both cold, and proud, and homely, and old-fashioned."

" She is a dear old lady for all that," said Caroline.

"Well, let you and I go and see what we can make of her, Lina," said Mrs. Wilkinson, taking her card-case from the table, and drawing Caroline's arm within her's.

CHAPTER VI.

AMUSEMENT FOUND—UNEASY DOUBTS.

THEY were summoned to the dinner-table the moment they came down from their call on Mrs. Hoffmann. Arthur Burnett also then came in; he was just returned from Mannheim, and was in the highest spirits; he had met with the Ponsonbys there; Bell was now handsomer than ever, and Tom seemed a nice sort of fellow. Mrs. Wilkinson's countenance expressed such unqualified pleasure, that Mrs. Palmer was sure they must be worth knowing.

"What branch of the Ponsonbys are they?" asked she.

"The Warwickshire branch," replied her friend. "Colonel Ponsonby is the brother of Sir John; we knew them in Paris three years ago, very dashing people." And then she went on to tell of their *soirées* and morning concerts, and blessed herself in the discovery she had just made of a musical genius, for she could thus in some degree equal her friend, who always had some *protégé* or other. "It was lucky, however," she said, "that they did not live in the same place; Colonel Ponsonby was a desperate gambler; a run of ill luck had driven him from Paris, and, in so small a town as Heidelberg, they might have found their acquaintance inconvenient, as it was now, nothing could be more charming; she would therefore drive over the next morning, and make her call." She then told Burnett of the musical

genius she had just discovered; that she was going
to give a little concert; and, now that the Ponsonbys
were come, she would invite them, and some of their
Mannheim friends also.

"Then you found the old lady up stairs not im-
placable?" said Mrs. Palmer.

Mrs. Wilkinson shrugged her shoulders, and said
that, like all Germans she had ever known, she was
extremely cautious—was very much afraid every
English or French person meant to take her in.
Caroline said Mrs. Wilkinson had been perfectly and
irresistibly charming; that she herself could have been
deceived into the notion of her having the utmost
reverence and esteem for her.

"I shall send her," said Mrs. Wilkinson, "a pair
of alabaster vases—we have far more than I know
what to do with. I knew, when I bought them, I
should give them away before I got them to England;
and really the old lady admired the figures on the
stairs very properly."

"She has very good taste, and a vast deal of infor-
mation—nay, actually solid knowledge," said Caroline,
"that only makes itself known by accident."

"You can look her out a pretty pair of vases,
Lina," said her munificent friend.

"I shall never forget," said Caroline laughing, and
turning to Burnett, "how amiably delightful Mrs.
Wilkinson was! I thought of all I had told Mrs.
Hoffmann about her, and I was sure she would think
that I had not spoken without reason."

"She is an adept in flattery and persuasion," said
he, looking archly at his adopted aunt; "and I shall
never forget a certain Mrs. Abigail Finch, who lived
somewhere in Holborn, to whom we used to pay visits:
—but, by the bye," said he, suddenly interrupting himself, and feeling in his side-pocket, "here is a letter

for you from Paris." Mrs. Wilkinson took the letter, and, while she was deeply engrossed by the contents, he went on: "Well, this old lady was prodigiously rich, and had all her money out on mortgages; and there was a certain Quito, or Amazonian, or Brazilian Joint-Stock Mining Company, that was rather short in its finances, and thought, naturally enough, that this old lady's money could be employed to far better advantage by them, pay her tenfold interest, and help them out of their difficulties. Not a week passed but the most tempting circulars went to her, telling her of gold, and silver, and diamond mines, and cent. per cent. returns on all money invested, but the old lady was proof against them all; nothing would move her, though a live member of parliament went to her. At last they thought of sending Mrs. Wilkinson to her, and I had the honour of attending her. Many and many were the visits we paid her, and many the bottles of ginger-wine and the plates of gingerbread we emptied; for with these dainties the good old soul always regaled us."

" And did she give up her mortgages?" asked Mrs. Palmer, with the greatest apparent interest.

"To be sure she did! How could she do otherwise?" replied he. "She died, however, poor old lady, just before the mines exploded, and proved to be only moonshine, and left in her will half the expected profits to an orphan house, or something of the kind; the other half to a world of poor relations; and the principal, munificent old soul, to no other than my eloquent aunt, together with her clothes, and fifteen excellent feather beds; which, of course, were all that ever she got, for the money was gone over and over again!"

Arthur Burnett laughed heartily; Caroline smiled, but she thought, though she did not say it, that such a story, if true, was not to the Wilkinsons' credit; whilst her mother looked very grave.

"What are you laughing at?" asked Mrs. Wilkinson, folding together the letter. "I was telling," said Arthur Burnett, "of Mrs. Abigail Finch's legacy!"

"Poor old creature!" said Mrs. Wilkinson, with the utmost indifference, and then added, "Mr. Wilkinson is in Paris still; he has, however, been to Petersburg. He writes in excellent spirits, and hopes to be here in a few weeks, when he proposes that we should go to Vienna for the winter, unless we prefer staying here. He says he has received a diamond ring from some Russian prince—I can't make out his name—which he intends for Caroline."

"How kind! how good of him!" exclaimed Caroline, thinking there never were such generous people as the Wilkinsons.

Mrs. Palmer said that dear Mr. Wilkinson was too generous; but, complaining of violent headache, said she would go to her own room and lie down.

As soon as dinner was over, Caroline went to choose a pair of vases; she was divided in her opinion between two, the one from an antique, the other modern; they were standing on the drawing-room table before her when Karl Hoffmann and Von Rosenberg came in to accept Mrs. Wilkinson's invitation. Caroline solicited their judgment; Von Rosenberg preferred the modern—it was, to his taste, more light and elegant; Hoffmann found more beauty in the purely classical outline and chaste ornament of the antique; Caroline said she should be guided by his judgment. Von Rosenberg looked as if he had received the highest possible compliment, in the preference given to his friend, and Hoffmann bowed.

Mrs. Wilkinson was delighted with the young

musician; to her mind he was the beau-ideal of a
genius: the fine contour of his countenance, the
picturesque effect of his rich flowing hair, the enthusiasm and ardour with which he spoke of his art,
all filled her with rapture; but when he sat down
to the instrument and played his own music, her
admiration was without bounds; she clasped her
hands, she wept, she nodded time to the livelier
measures, and foretold for him the most brilliant
career. "We must have you in England," said she;
"genius reaps such a golden harvest there!" She
herself, she said, would return to England for one
season, to patronise him; she had the power of making anything a fashion; she would take a princely
house in one of the best parts of London, and introduce him to everybody. Her husband, she said,
had unheard-of influence among the richest people
in the land; and, if he would only promise to come
to London, she would ensure for him not only a
splendid musical reputation, but a noble fortune
also!

Von Rosenberg, dazzled by all the lavish promises
of the enthusiastic lady, felt indeed as if the day of
his prosperity was dawning apace, and, full of gratitude, entered into the scheme of the projected little
concert with a zeal equal to her own. How happily
and gaily the evening wore away! Von Rosenberg
played unwearyingly; Hoffmann and Caroline sang
together as they had done in the days of their earlier
acquaintance; Mrs. Wilkinson applauded, and arranged in her own mind the plan of her concert, and
interrupted them perpetually, to communicate any
new idea as it suggested itself, or to call upon them
to decide between two rival ones; whilst Arthur
Burnett played with his dog, leaned out of the window to quiz those who were without, and then threw

himself on the sofa, to quiz those who were within; and thought that, spite of the enthusiasm of everybody, the evening was—to English a most expressive German word—very long-whilish.

All this time there were two discontented persons belonging to this associate household—Mrs. Hoffmann, and Mrs. Palmer. Poor Mrs. Palmer had thrown herself upon her bed in serious agitation and anxiety of mind, occasioned by the little anecdote Arthur Burnett had related of poor Mrs. Abigail Finch; but to her daughter she would not for the world have said one word of the true cause. "I think it is the heat of the weather, dear, that has overdone me," said she to Caroline, who, in the course of the evening, went to inquire after her; "you can send me a cup of strong tea; but one thing, Lina, I must impress upon you—do not be quite absorbed by this young Hoffmann; he is a very excellent young man, I do not doubt, but how is it that you always laugh so much more with Arthur Burnett than with him? You seem like a giddy thoughtless girl with the one, but like the earnest woman with the other; how is it?"

A slight blush passed over Caroline's face as she answered, "The characters of the two are so different; I find nothing to laugh at with Mr. Hoffmann—he makes me think; with him I always seem conscious of mind, and, like Undine, I suppose this very consciousness makes me grave and thoughtful."

"Caroline," said her mother, raising herself up in her bed, "you are unaware, perhaps, what your comparison implied; Undine loved when she became thoughtful; that is what I fear, that is what I warn you against; whilst you laugh, and are giddy as a child, I know your heart is unentangled: now, of these two—though nothing could be more improper than

a young lady bestowing her affections unsolicited—
how much is Arthur Burnett preferable to the other!
look at the style of the two; look at the fortunes of
the two—at their prospects in life —"

"But," said Caroline, interrupting her mother, "I
should hate marrying merely for worldly prospects;
why should I?"

"Why should you!" exclaimed her mother, growing warm and angry, "because it is your duty to
advance your own fortunes in life as much as possible.
For what have I lived abroad, out of my own land,
where all my affections are centered, but to give
you advantages which our small income would not
give you at home? You are handsome, Lina," added
she, intending to touch her by an appeal to her
vanity, "and have the style of a thorough-bred
gentlewoman. I have spared nothing in your education, as you well know; and it surely is but a small
request that I make, that you will not go and throw
away your affections on a pennyless foreigner!"

"My dear mother!" exclaimed Caroline, "have
no anxiety about me. I am beginning to be worldly-
minded, and, since our friends have been with us,
have acquired a very sufficient love of money, and of
the pleasure of spending it too!"

"Well, well, my dear," said her mother, pursuing
the subject of her warning; "and remember it is
often as bad to seem guilty, as to be guilty. How
absurd must you appear to the Wilkinsons—to Mr.
Burnett—if they suspected you of any *penchant* for
Mr. Hoffmann! how they would laugh at you! I
am sorry, for my part, that Mrs. Wilkinson has got
this musical mania on her, and I am sorry that I said
anything about Mr. Hoffmann's singing—it will bring
him here so much."

"Oh!" said Caroline smiling, "pray, mamma, let

not that trouble you; he and his friend leave Heidelberg immediately, and then we must depend upon Mr. Burnett for amusement; and dull enough, I doubt, we shall find it."

"Nonsense! child," replied her mother, "for you seem to find him always amusing; but go now, my head is worse for all this talking; send me a cup of strong tea, and remember what I have said."

When Gretchen took her mistress' tea she received orders to request Mrs. Wilkinson, unobserved by her daughter, to come to her for five minutes. Mrs. Wilkinson, in her enthusiasm about the proposed concert, forgot the request till near eleven o'clock, when the young men were gone, and Caroline offered her hand to say adieu, adding that she must visit her mother before she went to rest. "I ought myself to have gone to her," said Mrs. Wilkinson; "stay here, Lina, till I return; I have a little device for the concert room, which I want to consult you about; now amuse her, Arthur, while I am gone."

Burnett, therefore, who was by no means unaware of her enthusiasm for her German friends, and who, moreover, had been piqued by the preference she had given to Hoffmann over himself, began most remorselessly to caricature both him and his friend. He was irresistibly comic, and Caroline laughed extremely. Arthur thought her always lovely; he thought she looked lovelier than usual to-night; he was quite divided in his opinion as to whether she or Bell Ponsonby were the handsomer. Bell Ponsonby looked splendid on horseback; if Caroline looked as well on horseback, she was the handsomer, for Bell did not at all times look equally well in a room. He asked Caroline if she rode? She said she did; she had ridden a great deal in England, and liked it much. Burnett said he was delighted; he

had bought a horse for himself; his aunt wished **for**
one also, as she was fond of riding; he cared nothing
for riding out with her, and therefore he had said **he**
could not find a horse fit for her; there were plenty
of horses, however; and, now that Caroline rode, he
would go the next day and find one, and thus they
would have charming rides together; Bell Ponsonby
rode, and her brother had a most valuable horse; they
would make altogether a fine cavalcade, and astonish
everybody; he should not have cared much for riding
with the Ponsonbys, but with her, he assured her, it
was quite a different thing.

Caroline thought she had never seen Burnett more
agreeable than he was this evening; if he were not
positively handsome, he was one of the most gentle-
manly persons she had ever seen. There was something perfectly fascinating, to her fancy, in this unsparing indulgence of pleasure, unregardful' of cost;
it was as if the lamp of Aladdin were in possession
of the Wilkinson family. She thought how glorious
it must be, through the whole of one's life, never to
know the want of money; she asked Burnett if he
ever had deprived himself of a pleasure because of its
cost? and, while he is relating some of his most memorable extravagances, let us inquire what passed
between Mrs. Palmer and Mrs. Wilkinson. The
former lady was just about dispatching Gretchen with
a second request to her friend, when she made her
appearance, with overwhelming apologies on her lips.
" Really, Lina had been playing and singing so
gloriously, that there was no leaving the room; she
must confess having forgotten, but she hoped dear
Mrs. Palmer was not ill.".

" Sit down," said Mrs. Palmer; " for, though it is
late, I must have some conversation with you on a
subject of the most painful importance to me."

"For Heaven's sake, what do you mean?" asked the other.

"Perhaps you did not hear the anecdote which Mr. Burnett told at dinner, of a certain Mrs. Abigail Finch?" said Mrs. Palmer.

"About her legacy? Oh yes," replied the other, smiling.

"About her being over-persuaded—I think those were his own words," said Mrs. Palmer, "to invest all her property in some wild mining scheme or other."

"I believe she did so," said Mrs. Wilkinson; "but what of that? it is years ago; hundreds of people lost by the same bubble bursting; surely," added she, "you were not one of the poor old lady's disappointed heirs!"

"My dear friend," said Mrs. Palmer gravely, "I cannot laugh. Burnett said you were the means of this poor lady's calling in all her money, and so employing it. Now do not interrupt me," said she, seeing Mrs. Wilkinson eager to speak.

"I must!" said Mrs. Wilkinson, with angry decision; "Arthur is a foolish prating fellow! what does he know about this affair?"

"Nay, do not be angry," remonstrated Mrs. Palmer, who was one of those who always got the worst of an argument.

"I will tell you how it was," continued her friend, in the same overbearing tone of voice. "Mrs. Finch was one of those weak-minded women who are unfit to manage their own affairs; she was very rich, but was always playing with her money, as a child with his toys; now she would have it in mortgage, now in the funds, now in a banker's hands—she never was satisfied; and at last she heard of this mining scheme, and took it into her head to invest there."

"But pardon me," said Mrs. Palmer; "the mining scheme was Mr. Wilkinson's."

"No more his," returned the other, "than a hundred other people's. It was, like many another such scheme, unlucky; but what in the world has all this to do either with you or me?"

"Do not be impatient," again pleaded poor Mrs. Palmer; "and, if I am unjustly suspicious, pardon me; for oh!" said she, putting her handkerchief to her eyes, "I am anxious beyond what you can conceive! Heaven knows, but I have perhaps done as madly as poor Mrs. Finch!"

"You!" exclaimed Mrs. Wilkinson.

"I will tell you," said she, laying her hand on her friend's arm; "and oh, if you can give me assurance and consolation, do! Three years ago, when Mr. Wilkinson was in London, he was greatly interested about an Australian Land Company—of course you heard of it."

"Certainly, I heard a deal about it," said Mrs. Wilkinson.

"Immense estates of bankrupt settlers," continued she, "were bought up. It was a splendid scheme; the maps were laid before me, and even the company's books; I always was very exact in the management of my own income; I kept a debtor and creditor account with myself, and put down every farthing, so that I understood something of those things. I never saw clearer accounts than those that were shown me; fifty per cent. was the calculated return on all money so invested, after the first three years. It was a tempting thing. My daughter was growing up; expenses in England, as you know, are fearful; my property was funded, and my income, though certain, was but small; the temptation was great, and, God help me if I have been deceived—I sold out of the funds."

" Surely you did not!" exclaimed Mrs. Wilkinson, surprised out of her own discretion.

" At least," continued Mrs. Palmer, " Mr. Wilkinson, on whose judgment I placed the greatest reliance, managed all for me. I wished Lina to know nothing about it, nor does she. I have thought always what a pleasure it would be to surprise her some day with the news of our good fortune. Mr. Wilkinson for the first two years sent me quarterly statements of accounts, all clear and satisfactory ; for the last year I have had none. I was insured, for three years certain, for four per cent. on my money, which has been paid duly. I am in my last half-year. Judge then of my anxiety! I have the utmost confidence, however, in Mr. Wilkinson. I do not think he would willingly have let me be deceived ; but this history of poor Mrs. Finch has affected me greatly. God help me, if this Australian Land Company should prove a bubble !"

"Do not be anxious, dear Mrs. Palmer," said her friend, in the most soothing tone ; " do not have any uneasiness ; Wilkinson is a man who never engages himself in a doubtful concern ; he is lucky beyond example ; nor would he counsel you, for whom he has had always so high an esteem, to invest even a sixpence to disadvantage. As to poor Mrs. Finch, if you knew what a fool she was about money, you would only wonder that at her death she had any to lose ; but, pray cheer up ; Wilkinson will soon be here, and then we will have it all talked over."

" Hint not one word of this to Lina," said Mrs. Palmer ; " I am wretched when I think that perhaps I have destroyed all her prospects in life! I assure you, there are times when I think I shall lose my reason !"

" But Lina's fortune is not involved also, I hope?"
asked Mrs. Wilkinson.

" Why do you say *hope?*" asked Mrs. Palmer, with
eager suspicion. Her friend replied, that she had no
reason to hope or fear on the subject; it was merely
a passing question; she supposed Lina's fortune was
independent of her mother."

" Fortune!" exclaimed Mrs. Palmer, betrayed into
a confession she had not contemplated, ' Lina's fortune amounts merely to one thousand pounds, at four
per cent. interest—what is that? it merely buys her
clothes."

It was very little, Mrs. Wilkinson said. " Seven
per cent. interest on six thousand pounds," continued
Mrs. Palmer, " I have, as was stipulated, received from
Mr. Wilkinson; we manage to live very well on that
abroad; and I have spared no cost nor pains to complete poor Lina's education. I hoped to take her
back to England better educated, more highly accomplished than most girls,' and able to do justice to the
splendid fortune I had insured for her."

" Whatever Wilkinson recommended," remarked
his wife, " you may consider safe. I assure you
people bring their money to him, in preference to
putting it in the Bank of England."

" I will try to be satisfied," replied Mrs. Palmer—
" I will try to feel secure—but oh! I assure you I
have never known a day's nor a night's perfect rest,
since I signed my name to those papers. People
don't know what they do when they persuade others
to embark their all on an uncertainty! Now, tell me
candidly, as if you were on your solemn oath, know
you anything of this Australian Company?"

" I cannot say," replied Mrs. Wilkinson, " that I
never heard of it; but as to what it was or is, or what

it has turned out, I know nothing. Upon my word, I know nothing. I never trouble myself about such things; but when Wilkinson comes, of course you must know all about it. I 'myself think he ought not to have counselled your risking all your property; but, as he has done so, you may depend upon it the scheme is sure; and I think, besides, had any scheme in which you had an interest been unlucky, he would have mentioned it. As it is done with his advice, be easy; all will be well—I am sure it will; nay," said she laughing, "who knows but he brings you tidings of this golden egg having hatched!"

"I pray Heaven that he may do so!" said Mrs. Palmer.

"And now, good night! Make yourself easy," said Mrs. Wilkinson, giving her hand; "good night, I must go now and look after our young people, whom I left to amuse one another; I declare I have been sitting here a whole hour!" So saying, in a voice as cheerful as if there was no anxiety about money, or anything else in this world, Mrs. Wilkinson went out, to reprove her thoughtless, adopted nephew for having talked so unadvisedly, under any circumstances, but, as it happened, so unfortunately, on the subject of Mrs. Abigail Finch.

CHAPTER VIII.

DOUBTS IN ANOTHER QUARTER.

MRS. HOFFMANN had been busy for the last several days, not only in overseeing, but in assisting also in the getting up, of a large German wash. All this day she had been busied with two women, accomplished laundresses, in ironing her son's shirts, which, under her own eye, and with

the utmost exactness, was done this time with more
care than common, because this was the linen which
had to be packed for his journey, for his, at least
two year's absence in the universities of Vienna,
Berlin, and Paris.

Karl having seen his friend to his own door, entered the room in which his mother was sitting, not a
little surprised to see her up so late, for it was an hour
after her usual bed-time. " Sit down a few minutes
with me, Karl," said she, pointing to the vacant seat
beside her on the sofa. He knew his mother was
low-spirited at parting with him for the first time,
and for so long, and his manners were particularly
kind. " See there," said she, pointing to a pair of
vases standing on a commode, " a present I have had
this afternoon."

Karl rose and looked at them near; they were the
same vases on which Caroline had asked his judgment.

" They are a present to me from Mrs. Wilkinson,"
said she; " I see no reason why she should make presents to me."

Karl said that they were beautiful; that they were
copies of a celebrated antique. " I say nothing
against their beauty," replied his mother. " I only
wish they had not been sent to me; I would much
rather return them."

" Impossible !" said he, " quite impossible; it would
not only be ungracious, but ungrateful also."

" I shall not send them back, Karl," said his
mother; " but as to gratitude, I feel none. Mrs.
Wilkinson is, it strikes me, not generous, but lavish;
there is little merit in her giving, because I believe
her to be one who feeds her vanity by buying many
things, and then feeds it again by giving them away:
such a character would be unnatural in Germany,

but it is the growth of English extravagance. Such would give away whatever had lost its novelty, not from generosity, but weariness of possession; the receiver merely relieves them of a burden; there therefore can be little call for gratitude. Mrs. Palmer and her daughter speaks of her as so wonderfully generous, because she gives them so much. She would give as much to her waiting-maid."

Karl knew she was right, though he did not choose to confess it; so he laughed at her prejudice against the English, and brought one of the vases to the lamp, the better to observe it. "I am quite charmed with them," said he, "and will be grateful to Mrs Wilkinson, if you will not. You remember what Goëthe says: 'One should, at least every day, hear a little song, read a good poem, look upon some excellent picture, and, if it be possible, speak a few sensible words!'" said he, placing the vases on the slab of a low book-case, on which they looked extremely well; "there you may have daily before your eyes a design of great classic beauty, which Goëthe himself would admire. As for sensible words," said he, smiling, "you always speak them, except when you speak of our English friends."

"I have now your things almost ready," said his mother, thinking it of no use to talk further about the vases; "when you have made your calls of adieu, and such little preparations as you need for yourself, and your passports come, I think all will be quite ready."

"Are you impatient for me to go?" asked he.

"How could I?" she replied. "There is very little pleasure to me in the thought of being alone; but why have I busied myself so much, and even this day sat up so late, but that I believed you yourself impatient to set out? When does Max Von Rosenberg go?"

"Not for two weeks," replied Karl; "he has promised to arrange a little concert for Mrs. Wilkinson: of course I cannot go without him."

"I wish I was quite sure," said his mother gravely, "that there is not a secret influence, though perhaps you may deny it to yourself, which makes you reluctant to leave these English acquaintance of yours."

Karl blushed—yes, blushed—for a young German may blush without being ridiculous. "Mother," said he, with a kindness of tone which at once went to her heart, "take it not unkind that I ask you neither to suspect my motives, nor to pry into the causes of my conduct; and, as you have found me hitherto capable of judging for myself, confide in my judgment at least a little longer."

"I would not have spoken on this subject now," said she, "did I not believe you incapable of judging for yourself. Fly, my dear son, whilst you yet are, in some degree, a free agent! An English wife, Karl," said she, growing at once, as it were, desperate, "and a wife brought up in all the follies and extravagancies of the worst class of English society, is not fit for a German who has his own path in life to make. Dear Heaven! Karl, I am angry when I think of it! Such a wife as this would make a home miserable, were you otherwise the most successful man in Germany!"

"Your prejudices are so strong," said Karl, taking up his night-candle, "it is vain reasoning with you. I pray you to leave me to make my own acquaintance, and to guide my own actions, as I have hitherto done!"

"When I see you madly running on destruction," said she, "I will warn you. You have been more headstrong about these English people than about anything else! My eyes are open, and I can see. You are in danger, and I will warn you; and I will endeavour to interpose between you and certain misery. Upon that you may depend," said she, in a tone of almost angry decision.

Karl set down his candle again. "Do not let there be strife betwixt us," said he, in a tone which was calm, but betrayed emotion; "I pray you, by all the affection you have for me, not to urge me further on this subject. I am not a boy, to be turned about merely by another's opinion; this, perhaps, is the only subject of importance on which we think differently. I, on my part, promise not to be misled by mere fancy; you, on yours, must leave me to my own judgment—must put a little confidence in me. If I have not hitherto gone very far wrong, grant me yet this same liberty a little longer; ask me not any questions, suspect me not, but leave me with an unembarrassed mind, to be influenced alone by my calmest reason."

"Alas!" said she, "my fears were just—you love this English girl; but I will neither reproach nor remonstrate—I will only pray that Heaven may preserve you from the evil consequences that I foresee, and have foreseen all along!"

Karl shook his mother's hand, and smiled on her affectionately. "But I have one more request to make, which you must grant:" she withdrew her hand hastily, and asked what further he wanted. "That you behave not only with civility, but kindness, not only to Miss Palmer and her mother, but to Mrs. Wilkinson also," said he.

"No, Karl," said she hastily, and angrily; "you ask what I neither can nor will grant. Here I will stop; with these people I will have nothing to do; my intimacy with them is ended. I said so a week ago; I am doubly decided, now that I know what your sentiments are towards them. You must run

into what extravagant lengths you please, but me
you shall not drag along with you; I have done with
your English friends—I will neither show them civility nor kindness!"

Karl again took up his candle, and, without offer-
in his mother his hand, bade her good night. There
was nothing very extraordinary in it—he had done so
before; but at that moment she thought it unkind.
She looked at the carefully prepared pile of linen
which stood before her; she thought how she had
tired herself with working for him all day, and now
that she had pleaded with him, for what she believed
his life's happiness, he was angry! She lighted her
own bed-candle, extinguished the lamp, and went to
her own chamber, quite out of spirits.

Next day, Hoffmann and his friends made one of
their long favourite strolls into the hills; on his
return home, he found his mother busied in trimming
a cap, which she said she was preparing for a party
on the morrow, at the same time glancing to an open
note which lay on the table.

It was a note from Mrs. Wilkinson, inviting her to
drink tea with them the next day: her son and Von
Rosenberg had had their invitations the day before.
Karl asked no questions as to his mother's so suddenly altering her intentions; he merely smiled, and
said he was glad she was going.

CHAPTER IX.

NEW ACQUAINTANCE.

THE next evening, about seven o'clock, Mrs. Hoffmann, dressed in her best, and with her knitting in
her black silk bag, made' her appearance in Mrs.
Wilkinson's room. Mrs. Palmer was, as usual, reclin-

ing on a sofa, and apologized for remaining in that
position, on the plea of being unwell. Mrs. Wilkinson, her daughter, and Mr. Burnett, she said, had
driven over to Mannheim, and she wondered that they
had not already returned, as they had promised to be
back for dinner at five; no doubt they had stayed
and dined there, but that certainly they would be
back directly, as she knew Mrs. Wilkinson wished to
consult Mr. Von Rosenberg about her concert. It
was very strange, she said, that they were so long,
but as they had some old and very charming acquaintance at Mannheim, no doubt they had been kept to
dinner. Mr. Burnett, she said, was gone about a
horse which he wished to purchase for his aunt; but,
for her part, she did not believe, when it came, she
would ride; however, it was all very well, as Caroline could make use of it, and could thus practise
riding again, of which she was very fond. Mrs.
Hoffmann said, that in a university town ladies did
not ride on horseback much.

"Certainly my daughter would not," said Mrs.
Palmer, "unless she were properly attended. In
England," continued she, "she was always noticed
for her good riding—even in London, where may be
found the finest horse-women in the world." In the
midst of such conversation as this, Karl and Von
Rosenberg entered. "It was very awkward, very
vexatious, Mrs. Palmer said, that they did not come;
they talked of the weather; they talked of the projected concert; and then Mrs. Palmer rose from the
sofa, and walked to the window. "Oh, here they
are," she exclaimed, "and with them a young lady—
Miss Ponsonby, I suppose; a very fine English girl,
I hear!"

Mrs. Wilkinson, in her bonnet and shawl, entered,
declaring that it was impossible they could be for-

given; that the Ponsonbys had promised Bell should
accompany them, and remain a few days with them,
if they would dine with them. Dinner was to have
been ready at three o'clock—instead of that, it was four;
then the Colonel loved the table so much, and time
really went so fast, that she was shocked to find it
six before they rose from the table. She had not,
she protested, a word to say in her defence; she only
trusted to the mercy of her friends, &c. &c. Caroline
and Miss Ponsonby then entered, and presently afterwards, Arthur Burnett. Bell Ponsonby was, as everybody said, very handsome—a proud, although a
blonde beauty. They all three seemed in the most
triumphant spirits, and there was a great deal of loud
laughing and loud talking among the English part of
the little company, whilst the three Germans sate
silent and constrained. The subject of all this animated talk was the pleasure to be experienced in
their projected horseback excursions, Mrs. Wilkinson having deputed Caroline, as was expected, to ride
her new horse. Bell and her brother were to accompany them, and the whole country, even into the
Odenwald, was to be scoured; and, in spite of the
Germans who were present, Bell and Arthur Burnett
ridiculed the ladies of their nation, for their inexperience on horseback.

After tea, Von Rosenberg sate down to the piano,
and Caroline to the harp; but, through the whole of
this unfortunate evening, had she studiously resolved to
grieve her German friends, she could not have been
more successful. The truth was, she had been jeered
that very day by the Wilkinsons, for her German
tastes and feelings. Bell Ponsonby prided herself on
her Paris education and experience of life! and Caroline, afraid of being ridiculed, was ashamed to be
natural; besides which, the warning her mother had

given her not to be so grave in her conversations with Karl, left her not at ease with him; towards him, therefore, she assumed new manners—the manners least pleasing of all in Germany—those of a lively coquette. She was glad, however, when the evening was over; so was Karl, who now, seeing that poor Caroline had appeared to so little advantage, was sorry he had pressed his mother to renew her intimacy; whilst she, too generous to taunt him, thought quietly with herself, surely a few such evenings as these would make him willing to leave his English friends without regret.

The next day the new horse was brought home— a beautiful creature, and Caroline grew quite impatient to ride it. In the course of the next week, all the good villagers of the neighbourhood were familiar with the English cavalcade. Rich and poor all talked of the dashing English, who frightened both men and women with their spirited horsemanship. It became quite a fashion for groups of students to assemble to see them go by; whilst everywhere it was a question which was the lovelier, the dark or the fair beauty. During all this time, the projected concert was a subject of almost hourly talk in the Wilkinsons' drawing-room; a little programme was drawn up by Von Rosenberg, which promised to be delightful; Caroline, Hoffmann, and Madame Von Holzhäuser, all had favourite pieces allotted them; and almost every evening was devoted either to particular or general rehearsal.

The greatest possible intimacy subsisted now between the Wilkinsons and the Ponsonbys; there was such perpetual going to and fro between Heidelberg and Mannheim; such scheming of parties of pleasure; such balls and concerts, projected both for immediate enjoyment, and for the winter, if, as Mrs

Ponsonby hoped—for she had an immediate eye to Arthur Burnett, with his seven thousand a year—she could only prevail on them to stay in Heidelberg for the winter; or why not in Mannheim? The Wilkinson party had been introduced to the grand duchess, and been graciously received, and were now, together with the Ponsonbys, looking forward to a great autumn ball which she was about to give, and to which they had already received invitations.

Bell Ponsonby had been now ten days at the Wilkinsons'; Caroline and she were always together, and people said they were the best friends in the world. Caroline was sitting one evening in her own room, looking over a quantity of beautiful purchases which she had just made, in expectation of the grand duchess's ball. She looked anxious, if not unhappy: her thoughts were by no means connected, nor was the state of her feelings very intelligible even to herself; and, had she soliloquised, it would, perhaps, have been somewhat in this style.—"It is strange what an alteration there is in the objects of my pursuit now, and a few weeks ago! how much less I read—how much less I think—how much more regardful I have become of what people say and think of me! I am disturbed by the Hoffmanns' coolness, yet, what do I to deserve their esteem? I shrink from the Wilkinsons' and Bell Ponsonby's ridicule and railing, and do and say as they do, and seem to be guided by the very principles I despise! How ridiculous it would be to talk to them as I have talked to Madame Hoffmann! the worldly, domineering spirit of these people, would sneer down even the strong principles of Madame Von Vöhning! It is very strange what an unhappy, unsatisfactory influence Bell Ponsonby has upon me; she is clever, witty, sarcastic, and beautiful; I dislike her, and I fear her: I dislike her spirit

and manners, and yet, because I fear her ridicule, I
appear to have adopted the same manners, and to be
influenced by the same spirit. Both she and her
mother are bent upon making a conquest of Arthur
Burnett. Arthur Burnett, never till now, was of any
consequence to me; but I cannot let her triumph
over me: I care nothing for winning his affection, but
I do care for mortifying *her!* I must, I will win
him! I will make her confess, that a simple country
girl, such as she thinks me, who have never been
either in Paris or Vienna, can win him easily, whom
she wishes to win, and cannot! I despise myself for
all this; but it will do her good to humble her!" So
reasoned poor Caroline, turning over the white lace
and gold tissue gloves, and embroidered pocket handkerchiefs, without bestowing a single thought upon
any of them.

"I did not think," said her mother to her, the next
day, "that Mrs. Wilkinson meant to make such a
great affair of this, which she has always called her
'little concert.' I see she has been at work in the
dining-room, and she has ordered two thousand green-
house plants—I can't conceive where she'll put them;
she has invited, she tells me, no less than thirty people from Mannheim, beside the Ponsonbys; and she
has engaged ——— from the opera there, to sing."

"I don't think Mr. Von Rosenberg will like it,"
said Caroline; "he knows nothing of it yet—it was
quite a sudden thought of Mrs. Wilkinson's yesterday; but it makes him such a second-rate person;
and as the Herr Geheimerath's family will be there, it
will be quite a pity. She has altogether re-arranged
her plan; Mr. Hoffmann and I are dispensed with
entirely."

"I am glad of that," said Mrs. Palmer, "very glad
indeed; it made you quite too public; and, as Mr.

Burnett took no part in it, nor cares much for music,
I never liked it. We must, however, dress much
more than I intended, and that I am sorry for, especially as we shall want something quite superb for the
grand duchess's ball. I am sorry indeed about this
little concert requiring so much," said she; for she had
her own secret reasons for wishing to be economical.

Caroline, of course, knowing nothing of these
reasons, rang the bell, and ordered Gretchen to bring
in the large packet of purchases which she had made
the day before.

"I doubt you will think me extravagant," said
she, " but really when one sees people like Mrs.
Wilkinson buying so liberally, one is ashamed not to
do the same. I spent four times the sum I intended,
and, of course, as I could not pay for all, I paid for
nothing; so now I have the agreeable knowledge of
owing twenty pounds in Mannheim."

" Well, I think after Mrs. Wilkinson had persuaded
you to buy these things, she ought to have laid down
the money for them; it is such a thing to let a young
person run into debt! It's what I never did, Lina,
when I was your age, and I beg you will never do it
again; you ought rather to have gone without!"

" What could I do?" said Caroline; "there was
Bell buying the most exquisite lace, and embroidered
handkerchiefs, without any remorse whatever. I
know that both she and her mother think it shabby
that I dress so plainly, and I cannot bear that they—
that she, of all people—should make remarks on my
wardrobe!"

Mrs. Palmer fell into a reverie; she often did so;
and her daughter busied herself by putting smoothly
together the things, which, beautiful as they were,
gave her but little pleasure.

" I am greatly pleased," at length began Mrs.

Palmer, speaking on a subject which occupied her thoughts a great deal, "by what I have seen of Arthur Burnett; he is a fine young man, very much a gentleman, and rather singularly amiable, I think. I would be the last person in the world, Lina," said she, "to suggest that you should be at any pains to win a lover; a girl like you, go where you may, will never lack admirers; but one like Mr. Burnett— handsome, rich, and amiable—is not to be met with every day; you must be at some little pains to secure him."

"I am sure," said Caroline laughing, "both Bell and I make ourselves very agreeable to him. Mr. Burnett ought to be most grateful to us."

"I know," said Mrs. Palmer, "what is the secret spring of all the Ponsonbys' politeness and attention; one thing you may depend upon, Lina—all the family would be glad to have you and me out of the way— that makes them wish to get the Wilkinsons to themselves at Mannheim; but you must not let that girl outwit you. Sit down beside me, dear," said she, with almost tearful eyes, "and let me talk to you seriously. I have reasons which I cannot explain to you now, why I wish to see you prosperously married, at least with a certain prospect of being so. My health is bad, my spirits are weak, and the one wish and prayer of my heart is to see you happily settled. I have known the Wilkinsons for years; I esteem them highly, as you know; and I am sure that a young man brought up under their eye must be excellent; and then think, dear, only of his fortune, of the inheritance he will have at the Wilkinsons' death—it is quite a princely thing!"

Whilst her mother was thus admonishing, many thoughts were passing through Caroline's mind, which summed themselves up in this way. Hundreds of

mothers, besides hers, would naturally wish to win
such a husband as Arthur Burnett for their daughters;
Mrs. Ponsonby did; but she had already made up her
mind to be Bell Ponsonby's successful rival. Suppose, now, she were to marry him, what would be her
prospects·in life? She saw at once splendid city
residences, all the world smiling upon her, servants
at command, carriages, horses, handsome clothes in
abundance, no anxiety about money, a life of splendour and pleasure; suppose, on the contrary, she
married Karl Hoffmann, what then? She preferred
his mind and his manners infinitely to Burnett's; she
thought him much handsomer also; but with him
she could only expect the ridicule of all these her
English friends, with no chance of forgiveness from
her mother; and she herself must sink down into the
manager of a frugal German family, dressing plainly,
and counting the cost of everything. The prospect
was not inviting, and she could not help thinking that
her mother counselled not without reason.

CHAPTER X.

EVENING ADVENTURES.

WHEN Mrs. Wilkinson had extended her "little
concert" into as "brilliant an affair as possible," and,
on the impulse of the moment, had engaged ——, of
the Mannheim opera, and a whole orchestra of musicians and singers besides, she felt herself in a dilemma
regarding Von Rosenberg and his friend. She feared
they would be offended; but, as she had told everybody of "her *protégé*"—a wonderful musical genius
whom she had discovered, and whom she would bring
forward not only here, but in London—she still had
a wish to include him in her new arrangements,

although she entirely dispensed with his friend. She
sent for them both, and, with a world of polite speeches,
unfolded her new plans; first, as if asking their advice,
and then, when that advice seemed adverse to her
wishes, she said she must frankly avow having been
dragged, as it were, into an engagement with these
Mannheim people, and could now only solicit their
sanction of her new programme, in which Von Rosenberg was merely retained to play on the piano his
piece of music called The Betrothal. To her surprise
they appeared quite satisfied; Hoffmann said that, as
far as himself was concerned, it was much better; he
had wished before to decline his part in the concert,
but had felt delicacy in so doing; that, as he was
leaving now so soon, it would be a convenience to
him to be at liberty; he thought that neither he nor
his mother would be at the concert, as this would be
his last evening with her, as he and his friend proposed setting off the next morning; they waited now
merely their passports, which were expected daily.
One thing, however, both he and Von Rosenberg
objected to—the entire omission of Madame Von
Holzhäuser's name; she had been engaged for the
night; she had made all the rehearsals with them;
it was an object to her to be favourably known,
though she did not sing in public. With some difficulty, and not without Von Rosenberg threatening
to take no part whatever in it, Mrs. Wilkinson promised that she should be included, as usual; for, after
all, she said she liked her singing quite as well as ——'s,
and that, as Mrs. Von Holzhäuser must, of course, be
paid whether she sung or not, she should sing, as had
been at first intended.

These difficulties all got over, Mrs. Wilkinson was
in better spirits than ever, and the preparations went
on with renewed zeal. It was now the day before

that on which the concert was to be given. The
dining-room was fitted up in the most tasteful manner
for the occasion; there had been, for several days, a
sound of workmen hammering and sawing; and there
was now a great carrying in of benches and chairs,
and a nailing up of scarlet and blue cloth. Cuttings
of gold lace had been swept out into the street, together with many a shred and triangular piece of bright-
coloured cloth and paper, greatly to the enriching of
such wild-haired and barefooted children as amused
themselves with hunting for street-treasures. The
most gracious invitations had been issued to the
Geheimerath's family, and been accepted; and they
and the Hoffmanns were not only permitted, but
requested also, to extend invitations to their particular
friends. Mrs. Wilkinson had made calls on four or
five families who were considered the *élite* of the place,
to whom also tickets were presented; " for what is
the use of an entertainment," said she, "if one has
not plenty of people at it?" Garlands of flowers were
ordered for the walls, and the two thousand green-
house plants were disposed about on the stairs, in the
refreshment-rooms, and in the balcony, over which
was hung an awning of striped linen, and which was
to be illuminated with coloured lamps.

Nothing could be more satisfactory. The servants
of the house told of it to servants out of the house;
Mrs. Hoffmann's little Bena stole down many times
in the day, to get a glimpse of it; and she never failed,
when she went to the market or to the grocer's, to
report of what was going on. The families who had
received invitations, talked of it to those who had
received none; and, one way and another, it filled
the little city with speculation and wonder.

On the morning of this day Mrs. Hoffmann and her
son had been sitting much longer than usual after

their breakfast, in deep discussion, which became so earnest, and lasted so long, as almost to threaten the total forgetting of all usual preparation for the one o'clock dinner.

Karl looked ill and anxious, and as if he had passed a sleepless night. His mother imagined the cause, but Caroline's name was not mentioned by either of them. They talked, however, of the concert, and how that the Geheimerath's family were offended at the slight put on Von Rosenberg, and would now absent themselves. He said that he himself thought not of going. The truth was, he had now, after a painful struggle with himself, resigned all hope of Caroline; he not only thought that she preferred the young Englishman, but that he had mistaken her character. Such as she then appeared, such as she had appeared for the last month, and as she seemed studiously to wish to appear, could never make him happy—ought not, in fact, to have been chosen by him. The decision he had come to had cost him too much to be again risked. But on this subject they spoke not. They talked of the future and of the past; of friends whom they had known and loved, and who were now dead: they talked on subjects of affection and sorrow, which, suiting the state of both their feelings, seemed tacitly to ally their hearts in closer union. After this, he set about arranging his own small possessions—his books, and engravings, and music—as they were to remain, probably for some years; and then, leaving his mother to pack his clothes for his journey, went to assist his friend Von Rosenberg, who, by no means so methodical as himself, would, he knew, be no little obliged for his assistance.

What a confusion there was in Von Rosenberg's room! Clothes, books, papers, music, musical instruments, engravings, boots, pipes, lying about in the

most hopeless disorder, whilst his dog, which he had
threatened many a time to introduce to Mrs. Wilkinson, as a musical genius, because he had been taught
by his master to bark to the musical scale, sat in the
midst of all, with the most rueful countenance, as if
he were fully aware, as no doubt he was, that he was
about to be parted from his beloved master

"You are not badly off for shirts," said Karl,
arranging smoothly and tidily into the bottom of the
portmanteau a dozen of those useful articles of apparel. "Those same shirts," said he, "came into
my room, a week ago, in a most mysterious manner.
I thought the washerwoman had brought them to me
by mistake. I told her so: they had then laid there
several days: she said no, and opened one of them
in my presence; it was marked with my name!
Excellent shirts they are, and beautiful linen—I
never had such in my life before. It looked rather
absurd," continued Von Rosenberg, "to wonder before
one's washerwoman how one became possessed of a
dozen new shirts; so I said, very gravely, that I
supposed they were my new shirts come home from
making; that I wondered how I could forget having
ordered them."

"Yes, yes," said Karl, smiling significantly, "I
understand."

"And yet," said Von Rosenberg, "they pretend
to know nothing about it. Pauline says she has
been quite too busy to work for me ; but it's her own
sewing; nobody else could sew so neatly;" and he
very roughly drew forth another, to make his friend
bear testimony to the truth of his words.

"I am no judge of such things, indeed," said
Karl; "and, besides, it's no joke folding them neatly
again."

"However," continued the other, "Franz said that

both his aunt and his sister had been making shirts, and that he was sure she never took such pains for his father;—the dear girl! I wish you would look only at a wristband!"

" I cannot indeed, my good fellow!" returned Karl. Von Rosenberg said no more, for he had forgotten till that moment how much less happy his friend was than himself.

There was presently afterwards a rattling tramp of horses along the rude, hard pavement of the street. Karl was standing by the window and looked down. It was Caroline, Bell Ponsonby, and Arthur Burnett, followed by their groom, taking their afternoon ride. Caroline looked proud and happy as a queen on the day of a victory; she was triumphing over her rival. Burnett was close at her side, and was saying something to her which called a heightened colour to her cheek, whilst her bright laughing eyes avoided his glance; she looked upwards at the houses opposite, and through the open casement saw Hoffmann. They had not seen each other for several days. Whatever might be the expression of his countenance, a change instantly came over hers—an expression of surprise, and of deep and painful interest; it was at once as if the true-hearted, gentle Caroline Palmer had passed before him, such as she had seemed in the days of their earlier acquaintance, as she had won his love, and as she still remained, the beloved of his heart. Poor Karl! he had been firm as a rock till then, but that momentary expression unmanned him, and, no way ashamed that his friend should witness his weakness, he covered his face with his hand, and wept bitterly.

Caroline rode on, forgetting for a moment the gay flattery of Burnett, and her triumph over Bell Ponsonby. She wished she had not seen Karl, for she thought his pale, sad countenance would haunt her for days; she dropped her veil over her riding-hat, that the tears, which were filling her eyes, might not be seen, when, all at once, Bell, who had been rallying her on her sudden gravity, without receiving an answer, either intentionally or accidentally touched her horse with her riding-whip, and the creature set off on a brisk gallop. Caroline was an expert horsewoman, and kept her seat; but Burnett, who was terrified for her, sprang after her; Bell would not be out-done in riding, and they both dashed through the Mannheim gate furiously and abreast. At once there was a shriek, and a rush of people after them; but the groom only, who had not yet passed the gate, was stopped. A mob of indignant people at once rushed together; a boy, they said, had been knocked down and ridden over; some said that he was killed, others that his leg was broken, and all said that it was long expected that these mad English would do some mischief with their wild riding. It happened, fortunately, that the groom was by no means of a violent temper, and spoke German also; he said they were only riding to Mannheim, and would return that same way in a few hours; that his master was well known, and very rich, and would do all that a gentleman could do; but that now he must follow his master, and would explain to him what had happened. The people let him go, seeing he was so reasonable, and was unquestionably not to blame.

The poor child was carried away by one crowd, in which were more women than men; whilst another crowd, in which were more men than women, collected round the gate, intending to lay forcible hands on the English party when they returned, and conduct them to the Amthaus. Both Arthur Burnett and Bell knew that some mischief had been done in passing through the gate, but they stayed not in their riding for all that—Burnett believing that Caroline's horse had run away with her, and Bell being determined not to be out-ridden.

The brisk exercise and animation of this spirited ride had restored, in great measure, Caroline's gaiety; and her first feeling, on being overtaken, was pleasure in Bell Ponsonby's witnessing Burnett's anxiety about her. They had ridden to Mannheim merely for a bracelet of Bell's, which she wanted for the next evening, and, being ready to return, Burnett gave his purse, containing a considerable amount of florins, to his groom, telling him to return direct to Heidelberg, and distribute what was needful, on account of the accident, for that, as the evening was fine, he and the ladies would cross the Neckar at——, and return home by Ladenburg, which place they all had a desire to see.

The little Bena was busied in Mrs. Hoffmann's kitchen, washing and preparing a very nice salad, which would be needed for the evening meal, whilst her mistress was whipping up a rich raspberry cream, which, with a variety of cold meats, cakes, and tarts of various kinds, were to constitute a little supper, which Karl was to eat with his two friends, this being the last evening they all could sup together, as the morrow was the Wilkinsons' concert, when Von Rosenberg would be engaged. All at once, a violent ringing was heard at the Wilkinsons' bell; and presently, a peal not much less violent sounded also on Mrs. Hoffmann's bell. The widow started, and Bena ran to the stair-head and pulled the spring-latch, waiting the while to see who was coming. There was a loud talking on the Wilkinsons' stair-landing—all the servants were standing grouped together, and among them, sure enough, stood a *gendarme*, seeming **very** vehement in his discourse. Whilst she was making these hasty observations, a little wild-looking woman, with her hair almost shaken down with running, and quite out of breath, came panting up the long stairs.

"The poor lame Peter," said the woman, "has got his arm or his leg broken, or both; those random English people have ridden over him :"

Bena began sobbing violently, whilst the messenger of evil tidings proceeded into the kitchen, where she met Mrs. Hoffmann. "Those random English people," repeated she, "have ridden over the lame Peter! Poor creature, as it was a warm afternoon, and he had been sitting all day by the grandfather, a neighbour's daughter drew him out in a child's chaise, and, just as they were going through the Mannheim gate, the English, who were coming down the street, began to gallop, and dashed through the gate, never heeding who was passing at the time; the girl that was drawing him attempted to get out of the way, but some way the chaise got overturned—some said was knocked over—and there lay poor Peter under the horses' iron shoes, all covered with blood, and lying as if dead. Now you must let Bena come home for this night, for the mother is well nigh out of her senses."

Bena should go, to be sure, said Mrs. Hoffmann ; and then, giving her half a florin for her mother, she bade her haste away at her best speed, and compose herself as much as she could, for that, after all, it might not be so bad as she feared. The wild-looking woman saw her go, and, being tired by the haste she had made, took the liberty of remaining a little while to rest. She then went on to tell how poor lame Peter sate at home all day propped in his chair, close by grandfather's bed, and reached him, now and then, sups of wine and water, the only thing that cheered the old man; and how he would read to him for hours—for Peter was a good scholar, and so was the old man; and then, when the poor old soul was tired or wanted to sleep, how lame Peter would amuse himself with drawing; and oh! he drew beautifully, only he rubbed out everything when he drew on a slate, for they could not afford to buy paper; but that sometimes the gentlefolks sent him paper, and then he was happy! Mrs. Hoffmann knew that, for she often sent him both paper and pencils herself. There were some gentlemen, she said, who were wishing to get him into a drawing-school where he could learn to maintain himself. Mrs. Hoffmann knew that also, for it was her son's scheme, and was just about being accomplished. The woman said that he had opened his eyes while they were carrying him away from the gate, and had prayed so fervently not to go to the hospital, that they had carried him home, and laid him on his bed.

CHAPTER XI.

EVENING ADVENTURES CONTINUED.

The news of this unfortunate accident, as it was communicated by the *gendarme*, with an order from the Amthaus requiring the immediate appearance of the English cavalcade to answer for it, made no little sensation in the Wilkinsons' household. Mrs. Palmer, poor lady, was building up, as usual, a splendid vision of her daughter, as the rich Mrs. Burnett, figuring away in some great European capital, whilst her friend was busy devising an arabesque pattern to cut in gold paper, for some ornament of the concert-room, when the door was suddenly opened, and the valet and the French maid entered together, with the news that "somebody had been thrown down by

somebody's horse, and here was a policeman very
violent about it! What was to be done?" Mrs.
Wilkinson said she doubted not but that the man
wanted money; the valet, therefore, might give him
those six florins, and send him about his business;
what further was needful, Mr. Burnett would do
when he returned.

The valet came into the room again, balancing the
money on his hand, and venturing upon a smile in
the presence of his lady; the man, he said, had
refused the money. " Send him to me!" said she.
The *gendarme* entered. She was sorry—extremely
sorry, she said, for what had happened—the horses
were so spirited—but she hoped the poor child was not
so much hurt; she would send a servant with money
and wine immediately; that they would pay all needful expenses; and when Mr. Burnett returned, which
would be in an hour or two, he would certainly attend
at the Amthaus, for that this accident would distress him extremely. So spake Mrs. Wilkinson, and
offered him again the six florins. The man looked
for a moment at the offered money, as if ashamed to
accept what was, doubtless, intended as a bribe; and
then, perhaps recollecting that a bribe could be of no
manner of use, closed his hand tightly upon it, and
went out, neither looking pleased nor displeased.

" What a vexatious affair it is!" said Mrs. Wilkinson; " Arthur is always getting into trouble of this
kind He rode over a woman in London—a fortunate
thing for her, however. She was a poor dressmaker;
her arm was broken, and someway badly set; and I
assure you he has to pay her ten shillings a-week.
At Naples he rode over a lazzaroni; the man was
very old and ill at the time; I dare say he would not
have lived long, poor soul, but, however, he died;
and, as all his brother beggars laid his death at the

young Englishman's door, it became quite dangerous for Arthur to go out; I thought they certainly would murder him!"

"The horrid wretches!" exclaimed Mrs. Palmer.

"But there's a wonderful charm in English money," continued the other; "we distributed it freely, and presently, instead of our carriage being beset by a mob, cursing furiously, we were followed by shouts and blessings! I am sorry, however, that it has again happened, for it always brings vexation and trouble."

Towards seven o'clock, when it was getting quite dusk, the crowd assembled at the Mannheim gate were surprised to see the English groom returning alone. "Where are the others?" demanded they angrily, imagining that they were eluding justice. The man said that they had gone round by Ladenburg, and would thus return by the bridge; they grew suddenly angry, and began to swear desperate German oaths. The groom drew up at a wirthshaus just within the city, and called for wine. His master, he said, was the richest Englishman that ever came into Heidelberg, and that, if twenty arms and legs were broken, he could pay for them all; and that anybody who now chose, might drink a pint of wine at his expense. A deal of wine was drank, and then they escorted the groom along the street, insisting on his going down to the bridge, to wait for his master and the ladies.

"For Heaven's sake! Mr. Burnett, what means this?" asked Caroline, as they were received on the bridge by a crowd of people, who were talking of the Amthaus; "and why are we to go to the Amthaus?"

Burnett told her that somebody had been knocked down in the Mannheim gate—somebody drunk, most likely—that was all; that she need not alarm herself,

for there was no danger. The little city was all
alive; crowds were everywhere assembled to see them
go by, as if they were some wonderful spectacle.
Students stood in close groups together, with their
long pipes in their hands, and their dogs at their
heels, to get a closer survey of the two English
beauties, who were this time compelled to go at a foot's
pace. The Amthaus was lighted up, and there was a
crowd assembled about the door, which, in the uncertain dusk, looked greater than it really was. Caroline
thought everybody looked sullen and angry. The
gendarmes, who were walking about, drew up before
the door as they approached; they were ordered to
alight, to walk in, and answer for themselves. There
was a deal of uncertainty, for some time, as to whether
Burnett's horse or Bell Ponsonby's had injured the
boy. Arthur said he would allow no lady to be in
fault; and at length it was decided that all blame
should rest upon him. It was one Peter Heiliger,
they were then informed, who had been ridden over;
he was overturned from a little carriage, which the
girl who drew him attempted, but in vain, to remove
out of the way; the child lay upon the pavement at
the moment the horses entered the gateway, but no
attempt had been made, on the part of the riders, to
pull up, or to slacken their pace; the horses, also,
were put into a gallop at the moment before they
entered the gate. Several persons swore to having
felt in jeopardy of their lives—they had started aside
just in time to save themselves; an old person, or one
infirm, could not do so; and this cripple had been
ridden over, his life endangered, his leg broken, and
his arm seriously bruised. Medical men testified to
these facts.

Arthur Burnett, on his part, said that Miss Palmer's
horse had taken fright—that it was apt to run away;

and, seeing this, and being alarmed for the lady, he had put spurs to his horse to follow her; and that Miss Ponsonby, supposing merely that he wished them to have a brisk ride, had urged forward her horse at the same moment; that he was sorry for what had happened; but that he thought ladies ought not to have been met by a rude crowd, such as had met them on the bridge; that English ladies were not used to it, whatever Germans might be; that it was altogether an accident; that he would pay anything that was necessary, either to the child, or the parents, or doctor, or town, or anything," said he, growing angry, and only not swearing, because he thought it impolite to do so in the presence of ladies. The Amtmann told him that all that was necessary for him at present was, not to leave Heidelberg without permission; in fact, that no passport would be granted him, till the consequences of this accident were further known.

That evening, as Caroline, about half-an-hour after her return, was walking along the passage on the way to her own bedroom, she saw Bena, who had been sent by her mother, for an hour, to put away the supper things, as her mistress had company. She was looking, of course, very sorrowful, and her countenance bore evident marks of weeping.

"What is amiss, my poor Bena?" asked Caroline, who was always in the habit of noticing her kindly. At this question Bena began sobbing violently. "What *is* amiss?" asked Caroline again; "can I do anything to comfort you?"

"The poor lame Peter! the poor lame Peter!" sobbed the girl, holding her apron to her face. "Is he ill?" asked Caroline. "Oh, Fräulein!" exclaimed Bena, as if reproachfully—for she had no idea but that Caroline knew it was he who had been ridden over. At once the truth suggested itself to her; a sicken-

ing sense of misery came over her—the poor lame
Peter Heiliger was Bena's brother. " And is it indeed
your brother, then?" asked she, with tears in her own
eyes, " who has been hurt to-night? How grieved I
am! Will you let me go and see him to-morrow? I
will do anything for you; indeed I will, Bena!"
Bena thought the English Fräulein was very good to
speak so kindly, and she felt as if she loved her. " I
am going now," she said, " to sit up all night with
him, and we live in —— Gassè; and, if you are
so very kind as to come and see him, I shall be there
in the morning." Caroline said that she would not
fail, and, bidding the girl a kind good night, went
sorrowfully to her own chamber.

The long expected passports arrived this evening.
Karl opened them during supper, and, to their infinite
mortification and annoyance, found them incorrectly
made out; and now they could not set off for at least
ten days!

Everybody knows how unpleasant it is, when one's
clothes are all packed, all one's adieus made, and
one's mind wrought up into the proper mood for a
departure, to have one's journey deferred, whether it
be by losing our place by coach, eilwagon, or steam-
boat, or by having one's passport incorrectly made
out, as in this case. It is a very unpleasant thing
when one knows that one's friends and acquaintance,
on some particular morning, have said, " So and so
has a nice day for his journey; he must be just now
setting off; well, he is a good sort of fellow, a merry
fellow;—we're sorry to part with him." It is very
disagreeable to meet these same friends in a day or
two, and be saluted with, " And so you are not
gone, after all!" One feels as if they thought they
had wasted sympathy over one. One cannot expect
eve one's dearest friends to weep at a second parting,

although it be thè real one. After this, one can only slink away as quietly as possible, without a farewell from anybody!

CHAPTER XII.

RENEWED HOPE.

THE next morning Caroline rose early, and, ordering Gretchen to bring coffee to her own room, and to excuse her breakfasting with the Wilkinsons, set out on her visit to the lame Peter. When she reached —— Gasse, she met Bena returning to her mistress; the girl said she would go back and show her the way; —that it was a poor place, though the mother always kept it clean. It was a wretched upper-room into which Bena led her; there were two beds in it, partly concealed by curtains hung from the ceiling. It was clean certainly, but close, and filled, like all houses of the German poor, by a compound of strong unpleasant smells. Caroline, however, was in no humour to make difficulties; she entered cheerfully, and looked round; the curtains of one bed had been partly undrawn, and revealed the form of a very old man, who, but for the glance of his large hollow grey eyes, might have been mistaken for a corpse laid out. He was propped in his bed, and lay stiff and still, with his large bony hands spread out, feeble and heavy, upon the coarse home-spun sheet, which was turned deeply down over his bed-cover. He had evidently just been laid straight for the day; the hands, the head, had been laid there for him; he was too infirm to raise even his hands to his head. The eye, however, fixed inquiringly on Bena. "It is a right good English young lady!" said she; he was not at all deaf, for she spoke rather low, and the

intelligence of his eye showed that his intellect was
clear. "Will she not sit down?" said he, in a
low, hollow, and husky voice, which sounded almost
sepulchral; but Caroline was then talking with Bena's
mother, who, poor woman, overwhelmed with troubles,
and harassed and weary, was in no humour to receive consolation. The lame Peter lay in the other
bed, the curtains of which his mother had just drawn,
in the hope that he might sleep; but his groans and
his pitiful voice asking for water to drink, proved
that he slept not. "Thou must go now, Bena," said
the mother; "dear Heaven! what will become of
me?" "Give me the cup, Bena," said Caroline; "I
will sit by your brother a little while. Bena gave
her the cup, and, at her mother's bidding, after kissing the poor Peter, and bidding the old man good-
by, left the room. "Poor fellow!" said Caroline,
persisting that she would still sit by his bed; "he and I
are old acquaintance; if he could speak, he would tell
you so." The boy understood every word she said,
and, spite of his agony, smiled. "He and I," continued Caroline, "have known each other long. I
have had a deal of talk with him, poor fellow, when
he used to sit in the warm summer days, on one of
the seats in the Anlagen." He lay with his large
eyes fixed upon her face, and looked pleased. The
mother was mollified, and said that the fräulein was
very good, but that she had more upon her then than
she could well bear.

Two or three neighbours then came in. One had
promised to sit by the two invalids whilst the mother
took home some washing, which she was now unable
to do. Caroline said she would sit by the boy till her
return, which would not be long, and the neighbour
busied herself in some domestic work, in a little
adjoining chamber, looking in every now and then to

see that nothing was wanted, but not venturing **to** talk much to the young English lady.

Little did Caroline think that the pale, but interesting young cripple, that, very soon after her arrival in Heidelberg, she had noticed, was the brother of Mrs. Hoffmann's maid, much less that she should be instrumental in his suffering thus. Poor boy! it was that pleading expression of countenance, which is so peculiar to the suffering and the deformed, which in him had first excited her attention. She had sat down beside him on the bench, and talked with him; she had found him wonderfully intelligent; they had become friends, as it were, and had always, when they met, exchanged smiles, if nothing more. Of late, however, she had not seen him—had almost forgotten him, in fact. She did not know, however, how much he had missed her; how he had sat, and waited, and watched, in the hope that some of the handsome young ladies that went by might prove to be she. But no! Many looked kindly on him, but she came not! Poor Peter! he forgot his pain, almost, when he saw her sitting unexpectedly beside him; and, whilst she was thinking with herself, the lids closed over his heavy eyes, and he dropped quietly asleep.

Caroline let down the curtain softly, and then, crossing the room with noiseless steps, began to talk to the old man. He lay there immovable and corpse-like, yet with his pale and hollow eye full of intelligence. It was almost a surprise to hear him speak. In reply to her question of his age, he said he was not old—he was only seventy-eight; that he had been confined to his bed, and thus helpless, for seven years; that his daughter was very good to him, but that he was a sore burden to her—he knew it well; he wished that it had

pleased God that this affliction might have fallen **on**
himself, instead of on the poor lame Peter; it always
went so hardly with a cripple, he said, and Peter was
never strong. The old man was much affected, and
for some time he could not speak; at length he became
more composed. "Poor Peter," he said, "was so
clever, he might be able, cripple as he was, to do
something for his own living, and help his mother. He
drew very well; did the Fräulein see the pictures on
the walls?—they were all Peter's doing." Caroline was
astonished; for they were bold and very correct draw-
ings. "There was a gentleman," continued he, "in the
city, who had always taken a deal of notice of Peter;
he had given him instructions in drawing himself, and
had made many people kind to him, and now had got
him into an institution, where he would have been
well cared for, and made quite an artist of. It was
a long way off where he was going, but the gentleman,
who was leaving Heidelberg himself, had friends there,
and had promised to go and see him—it would have
been a capital thing for him." Caroline said that the
gentleman was very kind, and that she hoped, after all,
poor Peter could go. "Never, never," said the old
man; "I shall see him carried from that bed to his
grave:" and again, unable to speak, he paused for
some time. "He was to have gone the next week," at
length continued he; "the mother worked hard, and
saved a few florins. Some ladies sent him a shirt or
two, and stockings, and Madame Hoffmann"—Caroline started at the name—"a good lady is that! had
him measured, and all at her own expense, and an old
suit of Mr. Karl's—it was he, Heaven bless him! that
got him into the institution and did so much for him—
made up for him. Oh, fräulein, it would have touched
your heart to have seen the poor fellow in his new

'clothes—so proud as he was! and there they all are in that old trunk there; and there they may lie, for what need he will have of them!"

A few moments afterwards, Caroline was startled by the sound of Hoffmann's voice speaking to some one outside. She rose at his entrance; he saw that she had been weeping; he saw her confusion; nor was the effect of this unexpected meeting less evident in him than her. Few words, and those constrained and embarrassed, passed between them. She did not tell him what the old man had related of his goodness; she did not tell him, though she wished he knew it, how much she honoured his benevolence—how much she coveted his esteem; she said, however, and that with an emotion which she could not conceal, that one reflection made her wretched—that she had brought unhappiness under Mrs. Hoffmann's roof. She meant, at the moment, to little Bena; but she felt instantly, that her words applied with equal truth to others; she would not have recalled them, however, at the moment, for the world. Karl's countenance underwent an instant change He looked at her for half a second, and said nothing, but she understood what he felt—her words had given hope and happiness to his heart. He was glad that the passports were wrong; he resolved instantly to go to Mrs. Wilkinson's concert that night, and not, like a coward, to forego any chance of regaining her, if there were only left the shadow of hope; and Caroline returned home, determining to be worthy of Hoffmann, were it only for the quiet of her own conscience, and wishing devoutly that the Wilkinsons had never come, and that she had never known the Ponsonbys.

The moment she entered the house, she found everybody almost angry that she had gone out at all.

She was informed that Mr. Wilkinson had arrived; that he had travelled post all the way from Berlin, bur was now gone to bed, and would not get up till the hour for dressing in the evening; that he was going to set off to Strasburg the next morning, on important business, which would occupy him a few days, and then that he would remain here for some weeks. Her mother informed her that Mr. Wilkinson had not only brought her the diamond ring, but diamond ear-rings also; and that these, and the diamond cross which she would lend her, would be superb for the grand duchess's ball; and that Mrs. Wilkinson wanted her to look at the concert-room, and to try on a new dress, which she meant to have the pleasure of giving her, and which the dress-maker had been waiting to try on for hours.

Caroline ran to the concert-room, and found it perfect; she kissed Mrs. Wilkinson for her husband's costly presents; she kissed her again for the beautiful white satin dress—the very dress which she had wished for, but had been refused by her mother. She surveyed herself in the large mirror, in Mrs. Wilkinson's dressing-room, where it was tried on; and thought, for the first time in her life, she was satisfied by her appearance, and felt half sorry to think that Bell Ponsonby would not look half so well. What was her surprise, however, the next moment, to see Bell come gliding in, in precisely the same dress!—Mrs. Wilkinson had given a similar one to each. Bell looked wonderfully well that day. She was a *blonde* beauty of the most perfect character, with large blue eyes, hair like tinted silver, so long, and thick, and soft, and a complexion of a marble whiteness, upon which the blush of roses seemed to be thrown. She was strikingly lovely when animated: she never looked more animated than to-day. Mrs

Wilkinson said so; Arthur Burnett said so; for he was vexed that Caroline refused to ride. Caroline glanced at herself again in the mirror, and thought how haggard, and worn-out, and anxious she looked.

"You must look better than this to-night, Lina," said Mrs. Wilkinson, as they were sitting together after an early dinner: and, "bless me, child, how shockingly ill you look!" said her mother, as Caroline came into the room to dress, her chamber being wanted for a refreshment-room. "I shall look better, dear mother," said she, "when I am dressed."

"I hope so, indeed," said her mother, "or Bell will exult. I never in my life saw a girl so unblushingly bent upon gaining a lover as she is. I declare. it is quite disgraceful. Now, I look upon Burnett as all but your declared lover, and I think her behaviour abominable!"

Caroline never in her life bestowed more pains in dressing; her hair, which was not less abundant nor beautiful than Bell's, but of the very opposite colour, was, as usual, braided tightly upon her classically-formed head. She thought of the very first words she had heard Hoffmann speak, and she sighed as she thought he would not see it that night; for she had heard from Mrs. Wilkinson, that neither he nor his mother would be there. The toilet was completed, and Mrs. Palmer declared herself satisfied with the result; but still her injunction, again and again repeated, was, that her daughter should beware of the art of Bell Ponsonby.

The whole house was lighted up; sounds of music were already heard in the concert-room; people began to arrive; the drawing-room was full of the Ponsonbys and their friends; Caroline and Bell had each received a bouquet of rose and myrtle from Arthur Burnett, when Mr. Wilkinson entered. He

was tall and thin, of remarkably suave and gentle-
manly aspect. His high bald forehead gave him the
look of benevolence, but there was an expression
about his half-closed eyes, and the thousand wrinkles
that had gathered at their angles, and about his
closely-compressed thin lips, that gave the idea of
one who never missed his own advantage, nor never
let another gain an advantage over him. You might
ask a favour from him, but, the next moment, you
would be sorry you had done it. He was munificent, like his wife, but he always had his motives
for being so. He lived magnificently, and travelled
en vrince; but this was because he loved the homage
it brought him.

There was a murmur of applause when he entered;
those who knew him pressed forward to greet him,
and others were to be introduced. Mrs. Palmer was
charmed with his reception of Caroline; he gave her
his arm, and then, suddenly recollecting himself, con-
signed her to Arthur Burnett, saying that was far
better, and that he himself would have the pleasure
of conducting her mother to the concert-room. " It
is an understood thing!" said Mrs. Palmer to herself;
" I cannot have lost all, like poor Mrs. Abigail Finch;
or, if I have, it is thus they would make me amends."
She attended far less that evening to the music, than
to her daughter, and, as she hoped, her bridegroom
elect, who, to her great delight, seemed far more
devoted to her than to the gay Bell Ponsonby, who
sat on his other hand. She was proud to think that
others than herself might imagine it a settled thing
She looked round the room. and there was not, she
thought, a gentleman to compare with him; there was
Tom Ponsonby, who looked like a groom in his
master's clothes; there was a dashing Captain Jones,
and a Baron Von Elfinstun, whom many reckoned

handsome; but she thought otherwise. There was that Von Rosenberg, about whom Caroline said so much, with his long hair and Raphael-like face, leaning now on the music-desk, as if he took no interest whatever in the performance; and there was that young Hoffmann, whom Caroline at first had thought so clever, standing in one of the recesses of the windows, with his arms folded, and looking so intently upon something—she knew not what or whom, he stood so much in the shade; but what was any one of them, in comparison with Arthur Burnett, with seven thousand a-year, and such an inheritance in prospect!

In the interval between the two parts of the concert, refreshments were handed round, acquaintance recognised acquaintance, and many changed their seats. Hoffmann took the opportunity of exchanging a few words with Caroline, and, at the commencement of the second part, he was seated beside her. "Why, that actually is young Hoffmann sitting beside her, and to whom she is now talking so earnestly," secretly ejaculated the observant Mrs. Palmer. "What a fool the girl is!"

"Your daughter is the belle of the room," said Mr. Wilkinson, after he had leisurely gone the round of the apartment, and criticised every lady through his eye-glass; "upon my word she is!" Mrs. Palmer bowed, and was happy he thought so; it almost compensated to her for Caroline's talking to Karl. The compliment, however, was quite spoiled the moment afterwards, when she heard the same thing said to Mrs. Ponsonby—"Your daughter, ma'am, is unquestionably the finest girl in the room: I protest she is!" "Hush!" said Mrs. Wilkinson, coming between them, " —— is going to sing his last song: be sure, Wilkinson, that you *encore* it."

Poor Mrs. Palmer! she attended neither to ———'s last song, nor yet to the *encore,* she was so mortified by the words of the false Mr. Wilkinson. She wished she had not heard them. "One knows," said she to herself, "what a false world it is; but how much better to be deceived, than to know its falseness! Heaven help me! I begin to think that I may have been taken in, like that poor Mrs. Abigail Finch!"

It was a charming evening, everybody said—a most charming evening! Mrs. Ponsonby said she had not seen the arrangements of any private concert more perfect, even in Paris; she was, in fact, just in the humour to worship the Wilkinsons, so charmed was she with them—so charmed was she with Arthur Burnett, who, all the latter part of the evening, had devoted himself to Bell. In proportion as the Ponsonbys were triumphant, was poor Mrs. Palmer anxious and dispirited.

"What did Caroline mean by being taken by that young Hoffmann to supper? What did she mean by looking so pale and grave?" It was more than the good lady could bear.

"Have you and Mr. Burnett quarrelled?" asked she of her daughter, who, that night, the house being full, was to sleep in her mother's room.

"No certainly," said Caroline. "Why?"

"Because," replied her mother, " I could only imagine him turned over to Bell Ponsonby in some little lover's pique. Mind, Lina, what you are about —the Ponsonbys are artful, scheming people. You really have less spirit than any girl I ever saw! In a room like that, with the eyes of everybody upon you, and with your rival at your side, to give up voluntarily to her the best man in the room—the only gentleman whose attention conferred any dis-

tinction, for a paltry nameless German, positively
provokes me!—and when you know how much my
heart is set on this connexion!"

Caroline sat in her beautiful dress, as she had come
out of the concert-room, with her hands clasped
together on her knee, pale almost as the satin, and
said nothing.

"Are you a fool, Lina?" exclaimed her mother,
"or what, in Heaven's name, is come to you?"

"Let me confess the truth—let me open my heart
to you, dearest, dearest mother!" said she, bursting
into tears, and falling on her mother's neck.

"Nay, child, at least take off your dress before we
have any scenes," said her mother, in a tone of extreme irritation; and, as she had dismissed Gretchen,
that she might have this conversation with her
daughter, she unhooked her dress, and hung it up
for her.

Caroline did not again fall on her mother's neck;
she clasped her hands tightly together, and said
calmly, " I do not love Mr. Burnett—I hardly esteem
him!" More she would have said—she would have
confessed her love for Karl Hoffmann; it was the
confession she meant to have made before, but her
mother prevented her.

"Child!" exclaimed she, "what sudden folly has
seized you?—Not like him! you that have seemed so
charmed by his attentions—so jealous of Bell Ponsonby—that have made your preference of him visible
to everybody!—Not love him, not esteem him, even!
what in Heaven's name do you mean?—certainly you
will drive me mad!"

"Good Heavens!" exclaimed Caroline, confounded
by her mother's words—for she doubted not but her
mother spoke as others would speak also. A feeling
almost of despair came over her; she wanted some

strong-minded, high-principled friend to counsel with ;
she was hopeless of her mother; and, clasping her
hands together, she stood silent.

"Caroline," said her mother, hurried into a confession which she had never thought of voluntarily
making, and saying now what she devoutly hoped was
not true—"Listen, and then tell me whether you can
conscientiously trifle with the devotions of Mr. Burnett. I am pennyless! I have lost every farthing that
I am worth!"

Caroline stared at her mother in amazement.

"Yes, child!" she continued, "three years ago, I
was over-persuaded by Mr. Wilkinson, like that poor
Mrs. Abigail Finch, to embark my money in an
Australian Land Company. I, like her, have lost all
—only," added she, with a bitterness of voice, "I am
unfortunately alive to learn the miseries of poverty!"

Her mother's words were intelligible to Caroline,
but it seemed to her as if she were raving. Mrs. Palmer, after looking on her daughter for a moment, burst
into a flood of tears; Caroline soothed her, and prayed
for an explanation, forgetting her own troubles in
these new and unlooked-for ones.

By degrees her mother explained to her the whole
transaction, excusing herself by her wish to create a
fortune for her daughter. Caroline at first was indignant against Mr. Wilkinson for allowing her mother
to be thus imposed upon; and then adopted the willing hope that, after all, their surmises might be unjust,
and their money safe. She however besought her
mother to inquire from Mr. Wilkinson what their
true prospects were; which she promised to do the
next morning, before he left for Strasburg; though,
poor lady, in her own mind, she thought she would not,
as she was all along bent upon Burnett making proposals
to her daughter, before she ventured on the subject.

"The Wilkinsons know our circumstances, **Lina**," said her mother, "and my belief is, that they are here purposely for Arthur to choose you; I am sure they wish him to do so—nay, I almost have it from **Mrs.** Wilkinson's own mouth. They are generous people, Lina, and knowing, perhaps, that they have been instrumental in my misfortunes, this is the return they would make. Oh, Lina, if you knew how I have watched you two—how I have prayed for this union to take place—what sleepless nights it has cost me—what anxious days—you would not let any foolish fancies rise up as impediments; you must not, you ought not —nay, you shall not," said she, increasing in energy with every word she spoke; "for, if ever it was a girl's duty to obey her mother, it is that you obey me now! Think of the disgrace of poverty! Oh, Heaven! I surely could not survive it!"

There never was a merrier breakfast-party than that which surrounded the table as Caroline entered next morning. All the Ponsonbys were in such high spirits, looking so bright and unfatigued—the Wilkinsons, and Arthur Burnett also. All laughingly rallied her on her looks of katzenjammer, or cats' grief—for so the Germans call the weariness which succeeds a night of dissipation—which all said would, however, be cured by a new scheme of Mrs. Wilkinson, which was, that they all should accompany her husband as far as Anweiler, at the foot of the Haardt mountains, across the Rhine plain, the first day's journey to Strasburg—explore the scenery of the Trifels, the place of Cœur de Lion's captivity, and all the glorious country thereabout, down to Durkheim, where is the Heiden Mauer, and a great deal to see besides; and thus spend the time of Mr. Wilkinson's absence most agreeably, and be joined by him at Spires again, on his return. The Ponsonbys, of course, were to be of the party, all except the colonel, who preferred returning to Mannheim. Everybody declared it was charming—even Caroline was pleased, for she would have felt any change, anything which removed her thoughts from herself, a relief. It was just the excursion everybody had wished to make; and everybody said they were delighted. Mrs. Palmer, however, wished the Ponsonbys were not going, because Mr. Wilkinson seemed so wonderfully taken with Bell, and Bell really looked so provokingly happy; and Mrs. Ponsonby wished that the Palmers were not going, because, however doleful and unhappy Caroline looked, Mr. Burnett was engrossed by her; she began really to think there must be something serious in his attentions to her. So away they went that splendid autumn day; two carriages and four—Mr. and Mrs. Wilkinson, Mrs. Palmer and Mrs. Ponsonby in the first, and the four young people in the second.

The party stayed to dine at Landau, and then Mrs. Wilkinson announced to the young people, that they had arranged a very charming scheme—quite a new kind of pleasure—which they must enjoy the very moment of Mr. Wilkinson's return; and that was a musical breakfast at the Kaiser Stuhl. Mr. Wilkinson had noticed the tower on the hill, on leaving Heidelberg; they would go up there, and have a rural breakfast, and music. She would engage, she said, a band of musicians, and take that poor Madame Von Holzhäuser, who had been so disappointed in not singing at her concert; they would have Von Rosenberg also, and Hoffmann; and it would altogether be quite a snug delightful little affair. Everybody agreed that it would be so; and Mrs. Ponsonby declared that Mrs. Wilkinson had the finest taste in the world for getting up things of this kind.

It was with the greatest regret that Karl saw the

two carriages drive away, and understood that they were to be absent for a week. He had intended that day to have opened his heart to Caroline; he believed he was loved by her; he thought that, from their little intercourse the last happy evening, he had judged her harshly; and, with a sentiment peculiar to generous minds who have been unjust, blamed himself for his judgment, and longed to make the amplest amends even for an unkind thought.

CHAPTER XIII.

HOPE DISAPPOINTED.

THE party returned from the mountains delighted with their excursion, and impatient for the breakfast at the Kaiser Stuhl, which now had taken entire possession of Mrs. Wilkinson's mind, as the concert had done ten days before.

"Well, love," said Mrs. Palmer to her daughter, as they were alone together on their return, "I think the Ponsonbys must be convinced by this time, that Arthur Burnett has no thoughts of Bell. I never was better pleased in my life; I only wish you would look a little more cheerful, although I must confess that that air of melancholy suits you admirably!"

Caroline sighed, and said she felt sure she was doing wrong, but that she had not strength to do right. Her mother did not understand what she meant, nor did she ask her to explain herself, and she continued. "I am like some one before whom two roads lay—the one right, the other wrong; difficulties, great, untold difficulties, lay at the entrance of the right road; I have shrunk from encountering them; I have taken the other, though I know it to be wrong, as well as I

know darkness from light; and, please God that I
may only not know the misery my choice has occasioned another! I must be content: I have shut my
eyes and gone wilfully wrong! Oh how this thought
haunts me day and night!"

"Child! Lina, dear!" exclaimed her mother.

"I have made up my mind," continued she, "quite,
quite; and, come what will, I will bear it!" and, so
saying, she threw herself on the bed and wept. She
did not tell her mother what she knew, however,
would give her pleasure, that she had indeed accepted
Arthur Burnett's addresses. Gretchen came to say
that Mrs. Hoffmann had called on them, and that, as
Mrs. Wilkinson was out, she wished to see her, but
would detain her only a few minutes. Mrs. Palmer
went out to her.

Good Mrs. Hoffmann! she was come on an errand
of her son's. Her son and his friend, she said, were
setting off either on the morrow or the day after, and,
as Mrs. Wilkinson had often expressed a wish for tea
in the castle gardens, she wished to invite them to
coffee there that afternoon. Nothing could be more
delightful than the afternoons then were; the sunsets
too were so fine; and there was a moon now, which
strangers almost admired as much as the gardens; and
her son, she said, proposed also a stroll on the hills
afterwards, if it were agreeable to the young people:
there were some walks on the hills which he thought
they had not seen.

Mrs. Palmer, with the utmost politeness—for she
was in good humour with all the world—said she would
mention it to Mrs. Wilkinson; but she knew not what
to say, as they themselves proposed breakfasting at
the Kaiser Stuhl the next morning. A musical
breakfast it was to be; music in the open air was
always charming, and Mrs. Wilkinson got up those

things so well; she was then gone out about it, and the Ponsonbys also, most likely, as nobody was at home; that she expected an invitation had already been sent to Mr. Hoffmann, and Mr. Von Rosenberg also; but as it had not, she would venture to give it now, and to Mrs. Hoffmann also, whose company she was sure would give them all pleasure. Mrs. Hoffmann said that, for herself, she must quite decline; it was too great an undertaking for her. "But you do not decline, I hope, for your son," said Mrs. Palmer; "though, added she, "I doubt he might find some of the young people rather too much occupied with each other to be very good company."

"May I inquire, then," said Mrs. Hoffmann, "if the reports we hear of your daughter being promised to Mr. Burnett are true?"

"Certainly they are true," said Mrs. Palmer, who made herself quite easy on the subject now. "But, my dear Mrs. Hoffmann, remember one thing—an engagement of this kind is not publicly bruited abroad among the English, as among the Germans."

A change passed over Mrs. Hoffmann's countenance, and she rose suddenly to depart. Mrs. Palmer smiled to herself, for she thought she was displeased by what she had said of German betrothals.

Mrs. Wilkinson returned just before dinner. She had put everything, she said, in the right train. Arthur was gone about the carriages and horses; she expected him back every moment. He came, and his part of the commission was right also. She had issued, she said, a general order about provisions; and that, having met Mr. Hoffmann and Von Rosenberg, she had engaged them; that she never saw anybody more zealous than they were; that she was quite charmed with them; they had been with her to the musicians, and arranged with them much better than she could. Poor Mrs. Holzhäuser, however, made some little demur; her husband was ill again; she had lessons to give, and the mornings were cold. "However," said she, "as I should like to have her this time—for her voice will be wanted—I have offered her such a sum as I think she will not resist. All so far has gone right, but now comes the other side of the question: the wind has changed, and people foretell rain; and that child that has been ridden over is so much worse, that they say he must have his leg taken off. Oh, it is quite shocking! I never shall forgive you, Arthur. I heard it talked of in a shop, and it made me quite ill. I have sent Rosalie to inquire after him, and to offer them money, or wine, or anything else that we can give. I expect there will be a pension there, if nothing worse!"

Whilst they were sitting over their dessert, a note was handed to Caroline. Her colour changed as she glanced at its contents. Her mother, thinking it was a dressmaker's bill, and that she was annoyed, perhaps, at its amount, because her own finances were drained, told her where to find the keys of her desk, and if she wanted a few florins she might take them. Caroline hastened to her own room, and read again, with a heart beating violently, the words she had glanced over before :—

"For Heaven's sake tell me, are you indeed the promised bride of Mr. Burnett? Deal candidly with me. I have lived on uncertainties and hopes too long. I had given up hope till that evening of the concert. Why did you awake it again? But I will not reproach you. May you never know the misery I must endure!

"If what I am told be true, I ask not for an answer. It will be hard to bear, but, for my mother's sake, I will bear it. One request only I make to you—make my excuses to Mrs. Wilkinson, and Von Rosenberg's also. We shall leave this place to-night.—K. H."

Poor Caroline! she stood like one stupified, without a tear in her eye, and the open letter in her hand. She stood for a long time, as if pressed down with a blank sense of misery and error. It was too late to retrieve now, even if she knew how. "I forsesaw something of this," said she, "but I said I would shut my eyes, and go wilfully wrong;" and, falling down on her knees, though she uttered not one word of prayer, she buried her face in her hands, and wept. With even thoughts of prayer come a calming influence; and Caroline woke up, as it were, from that stupor of anguish. "Some way or other," said she, "light will break in; this tempesting of mind, this self-abhorrence, this dark uncertainty, cannot endure for ever." Whilst she thus thought, the regular pacing of footsteps in the room above caught her attention. "It is poor Karl" thought she; "he awaits my answer, or he knows now certainly that none will come!" She looked at her watch, as if to question how long it was since the note came; but she had not looked at it then; she knew nothing of time. "Oh my God!" exclaimed she, clasping her hands on her forehead, "this pacing to and fro will drive me mad! · I have made him wretched, without the possibility of making another happy!" She rose from her knees, and, with a sense of misery which had no words, threw herself on her bed.

That night Gretchen was not to be found when she was wanted. At length she made her appearance, and, in answer to the questions of her absence, said she had only been for a minute or two with Mrs. Hoffmann's Bena; that Mr. Karl and Mr. Von Rosenberg were gone off all in a hurry that evening, and she had just run into Bena's kitchen, to have a little talk with her, for that Mrs. Hoffmann was very poorly herself, and was gone to bed. Caroline said

her head ached, and that she was fatigued and would
go to rest; that Gretchen must offer apologies in the
drawing-room for her, and must tell Mrs. Wilkinson
also, that Mr. Hoffmann and his friend were suddenly
gone, and begged her to excuse them on the morrow.

Next morning was damp and dull. " Only one of
those regular autumn mornings, which turn out, the
most beautiful of days," said everybody; and, " Did
I not say so?" and "Did I not prophesy so?" asked
everybody exultingly, at ten o'clock, when the sun
looked through the misty clouds, and seemed half
disposed to disperse them. It is true that they were
to have been at the Kaiser Stuhl by half-past ten;
the musicians, perhaps, might be on their way there;
but that was of no consequence: the eatables and servants also had long been gone, and, now that all looked
promising, they would lose no time in setting out;
and, spite of Mr. Hoffmann and Von Rosenberg setting
off in that unhandsome way, Mrs. Wilkinson said
they would all enjoy themselves.

The carriages were brought to the door, and Caroline vainly besought them to let her stay at home,
on the plea of headache and former fatigue; but O
no! who could go without her? Arthur was peremp-
tory; he would stay if she did; so he took his seat
beside her, and away they drove.

As they approached the top of the hills, the air
began to feel damp and raw. Mrs. Wilkinson looked
at her watch; it actually was nearly twelve; had they
been, indeed, so long? and should they at last have
rain? But, however, they must not be faint-hearted;
everything was ready; everybody was waiting for
them; and, as they came in sight, a peal of music
burst forth to welcome them. There was something
animating in it on the wild hill-top, although the wind
did blow coldly, and the troops of half-wild, half-

savage-looking children, which had come up not only from Gaiberg, the Kohl-hof, and all regions about, looked starved; yet there was something quite inspiriting in that music, and in the servants bustling about, and the shed covered with green boughs, like a summer lodge in the wilderness wreathed with flowers, under which the repast was set out.

" And where is Mrs. Von Holzhäuser?" asked Mrs. Wilkinson, when they alighted, looking round for her in vain. A servant said that she had left a message, and was gone. " She was there at ten o'clock," he said; " that the damp of the hills had taken hold of her; her voice was gone; she could not speak above a whisper; she seemed very much cut down, and he wondered they had not met her." Mr. Wilkinson proposed that they should ascend the tower, and see the view; the man was there with his telescope. Mrs. Wilkinson said they would have some refreshment first; so all seated themselves at the table. It was really cold, and nobody looked merry, although the musicians played Strauss's waltzes and gallopades with all their might. It was a sumptuous breakfast, or rather luncheon, and, spite of the dreariness, ample justice was done to it; the gentlemen laughed loudly, and the ladies laughed too; the servants bustled about, the music played, the wild-looking children were regaled with far more than fragments; and so an hour went by, and by that time a thick, drizzling rain had set in, which left not, to the most sanguine, the remotest hope of a change.

It was, after all, the dullest party, the most complete failure of a pleasure party, that ever met at the foot of the Kaiser Stuhl. To ascend this imperial chair was now quite out of the question; the poor keeper of the tower stood at the door, balancing his telescope on his arm, but he did not even ask them to use it.

At three o'clock the carriages were drawn up again
for their return; the drenched and discomfited musicians had gone half-an-hour before; and, leaving
the fragments of the feast as booty to the keeper of
the tower and his children, they took their seats as
they came, and in rain, which threatened now to be a
deluge, began to descend, everybody silent and out
of humour. After they had dined, the Ponsonbys
returned home, and, tired and dispirited, everybody
retired early to their own rooms.

The next morning, Mademoiselle Rosalie brought
a message to Caroline. Mr. Wilkinson and Mr. Burnett were engaged together on business; Mrs. Wilkinson took breakfast in her own room—perhaps Miss
Palmer would do the same. There seemed nothing
extraordinary in all this; it was natural they should
wish to have some privacy, who had been so long
separated; but she felt now, as indeed she had often
done before, the inconvenience of this union of households. She was a prisoner in her own chamber, where
she had neither books, nor work, nor music; she
could not sit with her mother, who never rose till
late. She put on her bonnet and shawl, therefore, and
went to inquire, not only after the lame Peter, but
after poor Madame Von Holzhäuser also.

Peter had been removed to the hospital, she found,
for some days; he was now better, said the old man,
who was alone in the house; his daughter, he said,
was gone to the hospital with something for Peter.
It was a blessing he might keep his limb; it would
have been the death of him, so weakly as he was, to
lose it. "Bena tells me," said the old man, "that you
all live in the same house; you know Mr. Karl, then—
he's gone! It's much he did not come to say good-
by; but he knew that our good wishes went with
him, go where he would! I remember him," continued

he, "when he was a little boy; I gave him his first music lessons—I was a music-master then. Dear Heaven! what a loss it was to me when I could not play on my piano! I wish it had pleased God to have given the poor Peter an ear for music!—And so Mr. Karl is gone! he is a good heart—he is a right good heart!" repeated the old man, in his weak, husky voice. Caroline could bear it no longer: she wiped away her tears, and bade him good day.

In reply to her knock at Madame Von Holzhäuser's door, she was bade to enter in a voice the very opposite of the old man's—so harsh, so strong, so repulsive. It was Mr. Von Holzhäuser himself, who, wrapped in a dirty cotton schlafrock, with a greasy smoking-cap on his head, and his feet thrust into old faded needle-worked slippers, was puffing forth, from a coarse pipe, clouds of ill-scented tobacco. Caroline started back at the vision which thus presented itself as she entered the room: she thought she had made a mistake, and she said so.

"No, no," replied the stout smoker, who was evidently in ill humour, "this was Madame Von Holzhäuser's; that she had been such a fool the day before as to go up to the Kaiser Stuhl with some English people, who had more money than sense, and that she had lost her voice; and, now that Hoffmann was gone, who had been such a friend to her, what was she to do? He was gone off at last in such a hurry, he had forgotten to give her the recipe which did her so much good; and how could she afford to go to Dr. ——?"

The next moment a chamber door opened, and the poor lady herself, wrapped in a flannel dressing-gown, and with flannels on her throat and head came softly and timidly forth.

"May I sit down with you for two minutes in your chamber?" asked Caroline.

Madame Von Holzhäuser assented, and the door was closed against the unamiable occupant of the first room. The moment they were alone she burst into tears. Caroline said everything to soothe her and give her hope; to all the poor woman shook her head, or spoke only what was inaudible. What could Caroline do more? she could do nothing—nothing effectual at least: she ordered a quantity of manuscript music; said she would call sometimes; expressed the kindest sympathy and wishes, and departed with a heavier heart even than she had come.

Whilst she was taking off her bonnet in her own room, she heard a rap at the door, and Mrs. Wilkinson entered: her manner was constrained and peculiar: she sate down, and asked if she could have some private conversation with her.

"Certainly," said Caroline, her heart beating violently, for Mrs. Wilkinson's manner terrified her.

"My dear Caroline," said she, "it grieves me more than I can express, or than you can conceive—it is most painful, I assure you." The beating of Caroline's heart sounded into her brain, but she said nothing; and Mrs. Wilkinson, wanting a reply to help her onward, yet finding none, proceeded.

"I do not know, my dear girl, how to tell you—but perhaps your mother may have mentioned it." Caroline clasped her hands and leant earnestly forward. "Nay, do not look in that way," said she, or how can I tell you? Your poor dear mother embarked, some years ago, her fortune in a foreign Land Company —it has been unsuccessful."

"My dear, dear mother!" exclaimed Caroline, throwing herself into a chair, and bursting into tears.

"It is a most unhappy affair," said Mrs. Wilkinson; "but who would have thought of embarking their all in such a scheme?"

"Oh! why," said Caroline, "did Mr. Wilkinson allow it? He should not, indeed—indeed he should not; he should have discouraged it—he should have prevented it—he ought to have done so. Pardon me, Mrs. Wilkinson; but he, who knew so much of all money schemes, ought to have shown her how such as this Land Company, whoever may be the originators or supporters of them, are little better than public robbers. Her all! Oh my God! How can she bear poverty!"

"Who could have imagined it her all?" asked Mrs. Wilkinson, half vexed at Caroline's reproach on her husband. "He could not have imagined that she— that any one—would have risked their all thus."

"My poor mother has feared this," said Caroline; "these anxieties have preyed upon her health, and this blow will kill her, or deprive her of reason!"

"I am sure," said Mrs. Wilkinson, "I never was so shocked, so grieved, so miserable in all my life! I did not dare to go to her; it is the most distressing thing I ever knew. But bless me, Lina, who would have thought that your mother, who always made such a handsome appearance, and has educated you so well, was only worth six thousand pounds?—how did she manage?"

"Oh, Mrs. Wilkinson," said Caroline, "this has been unkind indeed, to persuade her to risk her all— her all, which was but so little—that little, which she made go so far!"

"You are sure to feel it," said Mrs. Wilkinson, in a voice which was meant to be full of charity; "I can forgive you being unjust; but, my dear girl, you must remember that your poor mother, and nobody else, is to blame. It is just as if she had taken her money to the gaming-table: people that do so, must abide the consequences. Why did she not tell Wilkinson that six thousand pounds was all she had in the world?"

"I must go to my mother now," said Caroline, rising.

"Yet a moment," said Mrs. Wilkinson; "a few more words you must allow me. Caroline took her seat again, and she continued. "I am sure, dear Lina, I am distressed to be the bearer of unpleasant tidings, or to have to communicate what must be painful for you to hear; but I have a duty to perform, which, however distressing, I must not shrink from. You knew, Caroline, though we did not, what were your circumstances—your prospects in life. You must have known this, and you should not have formed any connexion with Arthur, and have kept it secret thus."

"Mr. Burnett," said Caroline, looking both hurt and offended, "was old enough to choose for himself, and was, as I understood, independent of any person —even of a guardian."

"Unquestionably so," replied Mrs. Wilkinson; "he is very rich, but Mr. Wilkinson, from whom you know he has great expectations, has views of his own for him. I am very sorry, my dear Lina," said she, in the kindest tone, "for I never met with a girl that I admired and loved so much as you; but I must confess that I wish you had mentioned it to me."

"I have not mentioned it even to my own mother," said Caroline.

"So much the better," replied Mrs. Wilkinson; "and let me beseech of you, dear girl, not to do it. And now, Lina, I appeal to you—to your own good sense and knowledge of what is customary in society. I am grieved to hurt your feelings, by speaking so plainly; but knowing now, I say, that you must become dependent, one way or another, should you have accepted Arthur's addresses, without his obtaining his uncle's sanction, from whom, you know, he has such expectations?"

" I told him," said Caroline, at the time he made his declaration, " how doubtful our circumstances were —that I was probably almost penniless; he will not deny that. I believed you and Mr. Wilkinson capable of an act of generosity; I imagined you were willing to repay my mother's losses by this connexion: I was mistaken."

" Good Heavens!" exclaimed Mrs. Wilkinson, in a tone that seemed to express that the idea was preposterous; " then you know, love, I must speak plain, painful as it is," said she, assuming at once her most amiable manner, as if to cover the unkindness of her remarks; " if you had but connexions of influence, the want of money would go for nothing; family connexions, you know dear, are often better than fortune. Mr. Wilkinson—I am ashamed to say it—is very ambitious."

" I understand you, then," said Caroline: " you wish me to break off the connexion."

" I know you to be high-minded and reasonable," returned she, " and capable of the most generous and disinterested actions; I love you so well, that I would spare you all unpleasantness—Wilkinson is decided about it. I put it to your generosity; release Arthur at once, and spare him any breach with his uncle. Mr. Wilkinson believes—I will be candid with you, Lina—that Arthur has been inveigled into this connexion; he has had it from the Ponsonbys, I know; I am sure of it—they have been jealous all along and have said, I doubt not, very unhandsome things. But pray do not let it annoy you," said she, seeing the colour mount to Caroline's brow; for, poor girl, she remembered, with shame, many little arts of her

own, and many of her mother's manœuvres, to mortify
Bell, if not to attract Burnett. "I know how much
I ask from you," continued she; "But Caroline, you
are generous and disinterested; and, if you have any
regard for poor Arthur, and would spare him a rupture
with his uncle—and Wilkinson, when he is once
offended, never forgives—let the engagement be broken
by your own wish; as a woman, I counsel you Caroline,
it is far better you should do it than he."

"Let Mr. Burnett," said Caroline haughtily, offended by the heartless pride of these people, "ask
me himself to redeem him from this engagement, and
it shall be done. God knows," said she, "how entirely I acted against my own conscience in accepting
him; but I have accepted him: it is the sordid spirit
of worldly pride which makes you ashamed of our
engagement; if it be so, let him ask me to release him,
and I will do it! And now have I heard all you have
to say; for it is time that my poor mother was un-
deceived as to the friends in whom she has so long
and so blindly confided."

"Really, Caroline!" exclaimed Mrs. Wilkinson.

Caroline paused a moment, and then asked again
if Mrs. Wilkinson had anything more to say. She
coldly replied no; and they left the room together.

When Caroline entered, her mother was looking
over some papers which Mr. Wilkinson had sent in—
a hasty statement of the affairs of the Australian Land
Company. He wished, a note said which accompanied them, to have an interview with her some time
in the course of the next day.

"I can neither make head nor tail of these accounts
which Mr. Wilkinson has sent," said she; "frightful
sums of money seem to have gone out; but, Heaven
help me! as far as I can understand them, there seem
to be none coming back!"

CHAPTER XIV.

A RETROSPECT.

WE must advance on for four months, and, on one cold, intensely cold afternoon in January, look into a small, neat, warm room in a third story in the Neckar Strasse, or Neckar Street, Stuttgart: and there we shall find poor Mrs. Palmer reclining on the sofa, wrapped, as when we first saw her, in large shawls. The tea-things were placed upon the table, and Bena, Mrs. Hoffmann's little maid, had just brought in the lighted lamp.

"The Fräulein is not yet come," said Mrs. Palmer, as Bena set the lamp on the table.

"She comes this moment," replied she; and, as those words were spoken, Caroline in her warm winter bonnet and shawl entered.

"It is very cold! very cold indeed!" said she.

"Let Bena take your things, dear," said her mother. The kind little Bena placed the warm slippers before her young mistress, unlaced her boots, and carried away the bonnet and shawl, with a smiling, happy countenance. The mother and daughter placed themselves at the tea-table.

"How much better you look to-night, mamma!" said Caroline.

"I am better, dear," replied she; "and now you must tell me, as you have so long promised, the whole history of all those horrid affairs, in which I was too ill to take part, as I ought to have done."

"I think you can bear to hear it now," said her daughter; "but you must spare my going into detail, for it is too painful for me to dwell upon. You remember," said she, after a pause of a few moments, "that terrible morning when Mr. Burnett's note came in, and his uncle followed to second it:—oh Heavens! what a dreadful morning it was! I did not think then, that worldly pride could have been so undisguised!"

"Yes indeed," replied Mrs. Palmer, "I remember it; and that evening it was when I was taken so ill. I remember what seemed to me the roar of thunder, and they said it was the Wilkinsons' carriages driving away."

"Poor Mrs. Wilkinson!" said Caroline, "she wrote to me from Mannheim, where and at Baden-Baden, on account of the lame Peter's accident, they were compelled to remain some weeks, till a passport could be granted to Mr. Burnett; and then he bought his liberty for a hundred pounds—twelve hundred florins. It was, as Mrs. Wilkinson would have said, a good thing for him that he was ridden over. But I was going to tell you, that she wrote to me from Mannheim: the letter certainly was kind, and I am sure her intention in sending it was so. She had heard of your illness, and offered me whatever money I needed, not as a loan, but as a gift; she offered to get me a situation in London—in fact she did all she could do. The letter enclosed two fifty pound bills. Oh how sorely tempted was I to take them! I knew not what to do! God help me!—I had that twenty pounds to pay in Mannheim, for what I had so foolishly bought for the grand duchess's ball; there were dressmakers' bills, and bonnet-makers' bills, and bills for many a folly which I had been led into, by a spirit of rivalry and expense, whilst the Wilkinsons and Bell Ponsonby were here. I wished the money had been offered by any one but her!"

"My dear girl," said her mother, "that and much more you might have taken with an easy conscience: my money went to enrich, I make no doubt, Mr

Wilkinson and such as he, with their wicked Land Companies!"

" I reasoned so," said Caroline, " but I could not bear to receive what was given as a favour in our poverty. I returned it to her; I said that we could not receive alms from any one; that I would maintain both you and myself honourably and independently; and so I will!" said she, a glow of honest pride lighting up her countenance. "No, my dear mother, I thank Heaven that we need not live by charity!— I sent the bills back," continued she, " and took the diamond ring and ear-rings to Mannheim, and offered them to a jeweller there; for with these I said I will discharge all my debts. Good Heavens! I stood in the jeweller's shop bargaining about these things, at the very moment people were all going to the grand duchess's ball—to that very ball to which we were to have gone, and at which I was to have worn those very jewels; I saw the Wilkinsons' carriage drive past— they were going there!

" The jeweller confessed them to be of considerable value; he would not purchase them himself, he said, but he offered to present them at the palace, as, probably, they would be purchased by the grand duchess, or one of her daughters. In three weeks I heard from him; they were sold, I believe, to some lady in the train of the Empress of Russia; perhaps that ring might find its way back to that very prince from whom Mr. Wilkinson received it. I paid the jeweller his commission, and received nearly a hundred pounds; and that made me rich indeed. I went then to pay the debts I owed—in the first place, the twenty pounds:— it was already paid! I was astonished, and inquired by whom? By the lady, I was told, who was with me when I made the purchases—the rich English lady who had just left for Baden-Baden. I found it the same at the milliner's, and at every shop where we had gone together—I owed nothing!

"Gretchen left us just then; she had been quite spoiled by those English servants; and she went to Mannheim, to the Ponsonbys, I believe. Poor Madame Von Holzhäuser, cold as it was, and unwell as she was herself, came every day to see you. She was in a world of distress herself, for she could not give singing lessons for many weeks; however, she was my kindest and best friend; she sate up with you two nights—oh, how good she was! Careful as I was not to spend money, I bought from her a deal of manuscript music. I thought it was the only way I could return her kindness: but I carefully kept from her all my money anxieties; for I am sure had she known them, poor and suffering as she was, her generous heart would have refused the money. Just at the time when Gretchen behaved so ill, and left me at a day's warning, poor Madame Von Holzhäuser came saying, that in one way she could bring me good news—that I might then engage the little Bena, who had been such an excellent servant so long with Madame Hoffmann; that Madame Hoffmann had had a letter from Von Rosenberg, informing her of the illness of her son; he had been ill many weeks; Von Rosenberg had nursed him in Nüremberg, where they still were. Madame Hoffmann packed up her things in haste, sent the little Bena home, locked her doors, and set off for the winter to her son."

"Dear me!" exclaimed Mrs. Palmer, "such a healthy young man as he seemed!—But what is amiss, Lina?" asked she, as her daughter seemed sunk into a fit of abstraction, and looked deathly pale.

Caroline started, as if woke from a reverie. "It was a gloomy time," continued she; "an awfully gloomy time! I feared that I might become ill myself. Mrs. Holzhäuser and Bena were both as

kind as possible—so was Dr. ———; but I wanted
a counsellor; I had too much on my mind; I even
feared for my reason. I wrote then to Madame Von
Vöhning; it was the impulse of a moment, but it was
right. In a week's time that dear good lady was
with us. I candidly told her what our circumstances
were, and besought her advice. I had myself formed
the idea of leaving Heidelberg. I could not bear to
become the talk of that little city, in our humble circumstances; as it was, no one knew that they were
different to what they ever had been. I thought, if
we removed to some larger city, I might teach English
and French, and give lessons on the harp. Madame
Von Vöhning thought so too. When, therefore, you
were able to travel, we came here. I brought Bena
with us, regardless of the small additional expense,
because she is so good and kind, and I have, perhaps,
somewhat of a foolish attachment to the girl. She is
connected, in my mind, with the happy part of our
residence in Heidelberg, and she will talk unwearyingly
of good Madame Hoffmann, which I like.

"There is thus, you see, dear mother," said Caroline, "not much to tell you—all the rest you know.
In the spring, if you still prefer going to England,
Count ——— goes there as ambassador with his family.
They wish to engage me as governess to their children:
the situation is such as I should like; to be governess
in a German family, is to be received as a friend. My
only fear is, that you cannot live comfortably in England, on the very small income which we can raise."

"I would much rather," said poor Mrs. Palmer;
who, uneasy in her own mind, fancied there must be
virtue in change, "live on bread and water in England, than sumptuously in Germany; and, if it be no
very great sacrifice to you, dear, I should like you to
engage with the Countess."

"It shall be done," said Caroline, with a deep sigh, which, however, her mother did not observe.

CHAPTER XV.

ALL'S WELL THAT ENDS WELL.

THREE years have now passed between the ending of the last chapter, and the beginning of this, during which time Caroline has had a deal of experience of the life of a governess in England. The good Count and Countess ————, the friends of Madame Von Vöhning, returned to their own country in about twelve months, and Mrs. Palmer, worn out in health and spirits, and too feeble to travel, would not consent to her daughter's returning with them. She took, therefore, other situations, and, for some time, acted as daily governess.

We must see her now sitting in the room appropriated for her use, in the house of a certain very rich Mr. Paget Browne, in whose family, as governess to his only daughter, a great heiress, she had lived now for about six months. The house was a very large one, in the Regent's Park, and was, on the night to which we particularly refer, prepared to receive a large party. Everybody visited the Paget Brownes. On this particular evening, among others were expected Millionaire Wilkinson, as he was called, and his nephew Arthur Burnett, with his bride, the Lady Maria, sister of Lord Somebody; but the great star of this evening would be, it was hoped, the new German musician, about whom all the London world was mad, and who, it was whispered, had only that very week refused—and in a very peculiar manner too—an invitation from the lady of the Millionaire herself. It was just like these upstart foreigners, who come here as poor as beggars, and make fortunes like princes; but, however, it made the musician doubly the rage, and where he had had one, he had now three invitations for a night.

Mrs. Paget Browne, before she went to dress, looked into the room where Caroline and her daughter were sitting. "I have just had a note from Von Rosenberg," said she; "he says he will come to me to-night. I am quite charmed!"

"I did not know that he was in England," said Caroline, changing colour.

"For ten days at least," said Mrs. Paget Browne, not noticing her emotion; "did I not send you the paper, with the account of his presentation at court, and his concert, on Monday, at the Hanover-square rooms?"

"The real Von Rosenberg, mamma?" said her daughter, starting up in great delight—"Von Rosenberg, whose music we love so much?"

"Yes love," said her mother; "and I think, Miss Palmer, you must let Constance hear him. You will not object to accompany her into the drawing-room. It is not as if you were going in public," said she, not understanding Caroline's silence; "I would not ask it, only I wish Constance to hear good music."

"I do not object, indeed," said Caroline. "I was not thinking of my dress," added she, glancing down at the bombazine and crape which, poor girl, she had now been wearing about four weeks for her mother.

The great suite of drawing-rooms was filled with gay people. Caroline compelled herself to be calm, and stood in a recess of the room, with her fair young pupil leaning on her arm. She heard people talking near her; they said that the Wilkinsons would not be there that night. One gentleman said he would lay a wager upon it, because Von Rosenberg was coming, that Von Rosenberg had cut them three or four times, that, though the pride of these foreigners was unbearable, still they were glad that the Wilkinsons had been so mortified; and that Mr. Arthur Burnett would not come either, for that he was not particularly proud of his bride; that he had married her merely for her brother's interest, and now he was busy about securing his election, which, after all, he would lose, for that his brother-in-law, Lord ———, was not as strong in that quarter as they imagined.

But now, hush! Mrs. Paget Browne was crossing the room with the famous composer and violoncello-player, Von Rosenberg. All eyes were upon them; everybody said he was so handsome, and had such a gloriously intellectual head, and such beautiful hair.

"I must introduce my daughter to you," said Mrs. Paget Browne; "you have no greater admirer than she in London; she must dream of your music, for she thinks of nothing else all day!"

He bowed both to the beautiful girl and her mother. "Stay, Mr. Von Rosenberg," said the young Constance, who was full of generous impulses, and feared no one; "this is my governess, Miss Palmer, who knew you in Germany, and has told me a deal about you!"

He turned suddenly round—all eyes were fixed upon Caroline, who was pale as death. He remembered the English custom, which he and Hoffmann had liked so much, and offered her his hand. With a violent effort she commanded her feelings, and returned his greeting with composure. Amongst the gay and the titled, the poor governess, who but for the notice of the great popular favourite, nobody would have cared for, became at once an object of interest. She was questioned on all sides as to her acquaintance with him—his early life—his connex-

ions—anything that she could tell. It was qui'e
relief when silence was commanded, for that he was
going to play.

He played, and everybody went into raptures—those
who understood the merit of his performance, and
those who did not—for it was the reigning fashion to
be enraptured by Von Rosenberg's music.

"Do ask him to play the Betrothal!" said somebody; "for, though it is not new, it is so glorious!"

"He has been asked," said another; "I heard him
asked by three several persons, and he said that to-
night he could not play it!"

"How odd!" said a third.

It made quite a sensation in the house the next day,
when Von Rosenberg called, not only on Mrs. Pag t
Browne, but on the poor governess also. They talked
about old times; about Pauline, and the good old
Geheimerath, who, Von Rosenberg said, had invited
him to return for the Christmas Eve; and of course
he should do so—his lehre-jahre would then, he
hoped, be completed; but he knew not—the Geheimerath was a stern task-master. They talked about
Madame Hoffmann—Von Rosenberg talked of Karl—
Caroline felt as if she could not mention his name;
he told of his illness in Nüremberg, and of the winter
they spent there. Madame Hoffmann, he said, was
now living just as she used to do, in her old dwelling
in Heidelberg; he doubted not but even that little
Bena was with her. Karl, he said, had just been there,
but that he was now gone to live at Berlin, being
especially invited there by the young king, who was
bent upon gathering around him the most celebrated
and promising minds of Germany. He himself, he
said, had an invitation also to reside there, but Pauline must decide for him. Hoffmann, he said, it was
probable would before long come over to England;

he had, he said, written to him that very morning,
urging him to come whilst he was there.

How busy everybody is before Christmas-Eve in
Germany! All the land through, from the palace of
the Kaiser, down to the cottage of the poorest peasant, every one, old and young, is preparing a gift,
the best he can make, the one which he thinks will be
liked best, for each one that he loves. Walk through
any town or city of Germany, from one end of the
land to the other, and on Christmas-Eve in every
home is rejoicing. Through the unshuttered windows
you see the rooms lighted up, as if for a general illu-
mination—it is the Christ-tree, bearing its thousand
tapers, and shining out, a vision of beauty, casting
down light and splendour upon the gifts which lie
spread abroad below. From every house is heard
sounds of gladness—the bursting laugh of delighted
and astonished children—whilst parents and friends
stand by with tearful eyes, and hearts overflowing
with love.

It is a blessed night—it is the one night throughout
the year, in which, most emphatically, the broad wings
of universal love overshadow all things! They say
that the angelic Christ-child is gone forth with his
shining wings, the emblem of the great Christian spirit,
diffusing peace and joy, and good-will, and showering
down gifts upon all! They have said truly; their
hearts have received him with all the simplicity and
faith of little children; they have brought the great
spirit of love down to their own firesides, and, the
whole year through, they experience the blessing of it!

What busy preparation then was there in the dwelling of the Geheimerath Damian, for many days before
the Christmas-Eve of 1840!

The Herr Geheimerath and his sister called one day

on Mrs. Hoffmann. "You must hold your Christ-mas-Eve with us," said he; you must come to us with all your gifts and your rejoicings; our young people are all very busy; Von Rosenberg comes, as you know, but Pauline knows nothing of it."

The aunt said that she had bought the tree—a tree of unusual dimensions, because she expected it had that year to overshadow extraordinary gifts. Bena, she said, must come and help to ornament it; that the lame Peter, who was come home for his Christmas, and was wonderfully improved every way, was to be there; he had, she said, gifts of his own to present, especially to Karl's young wife, for whom he had great affection; she had seen the poor fellow's gifts, she said, but of course she could say no more; that he had also various little devices for the tree, which charmed her much, and he was to come and help for several days.

Mrs. Hoffmann received a letter three days before Christmas-Eve, written from Aix-la-Chapelle: it was from Karl. He said that he and his wife, and Von Rosenberg, had travelled thus far on their journey, and, spite of the season, all had been pleasant and prosperous; that assuredly, on the day before Christ-mas-Eve, they would present themselves, but not before, as the Herr Geheimerath had forbidden it. They should take their time, and arrive unfatigued by travelling, that they might all enjoy the Christmas-Eve thoroughly. Caroline added something to the letter, which pleased the good lady no little; for the German in which it was expressed, was pure as that of a native; the calligraphy too was German, and the sentiments those of the most cordial affection—worthy, said the kind mother-in-law, of the warmest German heart.

"Well," said she, to Madame Von Holzhäuser, with whom things were once more going on tolerably

smoothly. "he said he would enrich me this Christmas
with a noble gift; he will do so indeed, if this my
new daughter be only half what he and Von Rosenberg tell me : but you are invited to the Herr Geheimerath's," said she.

Madame Von Holzhäuser wiped her eyes, and said
it made her weep to think what the Frau Doctorin's
(Mrs. Karl's) feelings would be, on returning thus
to all her old acquaintance; but, as to her going to the
Herr Geheimerath's, that could not be; she always
kept a little Christmas at home; her husband she said,
would expect it—it was one of the few things which
put him in really good humour; and she did not know
exactly, but she thought he had been making some
little preparation of his own for it.

Mrs. Hoffmann gave her her hand, and said how
much pleased she was to hear it.

On the evening of the 23rd of December, a carriage
drove into Heidelberg, through the Mannheim gate.
It was cold, bitterly cold, that evening, as everybody
may remember. The postilion came on blowing his
horn, which sounded loud and shrill in the clear,
frosty air. The carriage passed the house of the
Herr Geheimerath, and up the street, drawing up at
last before the door of the house where Madame Hoffmann was still a dweller. Happy Caroline! Did
she think of that summer evening, when she first saw
Karl and his friends arrive at that very door? Perhaps she did. Bena stood on the stairs with a candle,
and Mrs. Hoffmann, dressed so nicely, came out to
meet them at her sitting-room door.

"Welcome, my daughter," said she, kissing her
most affectionately.

Caroline returned the kiss, but her heart was too
full to speak.

About an hour afterwards, when all their travelling

things were taken off, and they were sitting happily
together at tea, the good Geheimerath walked in.
" I am not come to stay," said he, " only to bid you
welcome, and to know that you are all well. Feldmann is at the door," said he, " but he will not com
in." Von Rosenberg went out and compelled their
merry-hearted friend to enter. "Only one quarter of
an hour," said the good old man, taking out his
watch, "will we stay with you."

The great drawing-room, or saloon as it was called,
in the Herr Geheimerath's house, was closed, as if
with seven seals and twice seven locks, excepting to
two persons—the lame Peter, who had the ordering
of all the lesser arrangements, and the good aunt, to
whom the Geheimerath himself, and all the rest of
the family, committed gifts and important secrets.

About four o'clock, when it was getting dusk, she
and Peter were observed to come out of the saloon
with very self-satisfied faces, as if all their work was
done.

" Is all ready?" inquired the younger voices.

"No, no; to be sure, not till it is quite dark,"
said the elder ones.

At last it grew dark, and then Peter and the aunt
went in again with lighted candles. The family, all
dressed in their best, were assembled in the adjoining
room, which opened into the saloon. Madame Hoffmann was there, and kindly welcomed by all. There
stood Karl and his English wife. Von Rosenberg
was not there ; none of the Hoffmanns had seen him
for all the afternoon; they wondered where he was,
but they did not ask, for they had the Geheimerath's
injunction of silence.

The children declared that the Christ-child must
have entered, for that light shone through the cracks
of the door. Their father quietly extinguished the

.amp in the room where they were, and then, indeed, bright lines of light were visible.

" Hush!" said the Geheimerath, and the two large folding-doors slowly opened and revealed the dazzling temple of the Christ-child.   Aloft stood the blazing tree, shining with its hundreds of lights, and bearing its glittering fruit of sugar-work.   Hundreds of little tapers flamed from among the green moss which edged the tables on which the gifts of so many loving hearts were displayed.   Nobody was forgotten—neither Madame Von Holzhäuser, though she was not there, nor the bed-ridden grandfather, nor the little Bena; and Peter saw, though he had no idea of it before, that the good aunt had her little corner of mystery also covered up with a cloth.

Caroline leaned on the arm of her husband, and smiled with tearful eyes, blessing in her soul this warm-hearted German land, which, with all its wisdom and philosophy, has preserved so much child-like simplicity in its heart.

The Herr Geheimerath came forward; there was a smile on his face of the most affectionate happiness He took Pauline by the hand, and led her towards the Christ-tree, behind which hung a long crimson curtain

" Lift that curtain," said he, " and there thou will find my gift to thee."

· She lifted it, or rather, it was lifted at the same moment, and Von Rosenberg clasped her in his arms

"Thy year of probation is ended!" said the good father; "receive thy wife!   Pauline, my blessing be on thee! receive thy husband!"

THE END.

www.ingramcontent.com/pod-product-compliance
Lightning Source LLC
Chambersburg PA
CBHW022355020726
47500CB00002B/283